DANCER IN LINGERIE

LINGERIE #13

PENELOPE SKY

CONTENTS

1. Carmen   1
2. Bosco   21
3. Carmen   27
4. Bosco   59
5. Carmen   77
6. Bosco   103
7. Carmen   115
8. Bosco   145
9. Carmen   171
10. Bosco   207
11. Carmen   229
12. Bosco   243
13. Carmen   247

Also by Penelope Sky   259

1

CARMEN

WE FINISHED dinner at the restaurant then walked out into the winter air. The frigid temperature struck my skin the second we were outside, and I buttoned up my long black coat to protect my skin in the tight dress I wore. Knee-high boots were on my feet, protecting my skin to my knees. My stomach was warm from the wine and hot food, so that acted as an extra buffer from the nighttime chill.

Griffin had his arm around Vanessa as we reached the sidewalk. In a black blazer with a V-neck on underneath, he didn't look like the psycho badass who had ink all over his body. The only thing visible now was the black ink on his left hand—his vow of eternal love.

He took off his jacket and immediately wrapped it around Vanessa, even though she was in a long-sleeved black cotton dress. Her baby bump was noticeable, even when she wore all black.

"I'm not cold," she said quietly to him as the jacket sat on her shoulders.

"Don't care." He wrapped it around her and stood behind her, keeping the jacket secure around her body as his hand moved to her bump. His hands were enormous, and it was easy for him to span her small pregnant belly with just a single palm.

She rolled her eyes, but the love was written all over her face. Her annoyance wasn't real, and right before my eyes, she fell in love with him even deeper.

Seeing them together only convinced me of what I wanted someday. I wanted a passionate love like theirs, a man who loved me so much that he would die for me—a thousand times. And I wanted a man I would take a bullet for—because I couldn't live without him. As a woman in her midtwenties, I was having fun and meeting new people every weekend. But now that I'd witnessed their love, I was starting to crave something more. Real love wasn't something you just found on the street corner—it found you. My time would come eventually, but it might not be for years.

"That bump is so cute, Vanessa." I smiled at her, seeing my cousin glow in the height of winter. "I can't wait until we have another little Barsetti running around."

She rested her hand on his as she leaned against him. "Me too."

Griffin kissed her on the cheek. "I love this bump. Sexy." He kissed her neck before he pulled away. "I'll get the car." He never cared about his overwhelming public display of affection for her, even in front of her family.

But that only made me like him more.

Vanessa stepped closer to me, keeping his jacket wrapped around her. "Dinner was nice."

"The bread they have here is the best. I was on a date here last weekend, and I ate the whole basket by myself."

Vanessa chuckled. "What did the guy think?"

I shrugged. "I don't care."

She smiled. "Good answer."

Griffin pulled up in his truck, then came around to the passenger side and got the door open. "Come on, baby. The car is warmed up."

"Let's go," Vanessa said to me as she let Griffin help her into the seat.

"I don't need a ride. My apartment is just two blocks away." It would take me less time to walk there than it would for them to drive me.

Griffin looked at me like I'd just insulted him. "Get. In."

"No. Thank. You." I smiled, loving the way he got so worked up so quickly. "It's a one-way street. You're gonna have to loop back around, which seems silly since my apartment is literally right there."

His nostrils flared like a provoked bull. "Don't make me ask you again."

"I thought you told my father I could handle myself?" Griffin had always respected me as a person, not just a woman. But ever since he married Vanessa, he'd started to behave like an overprotective big brother.

"Yes," he answered with a clenched jaw. "That has nothing to do with this."

"Get your pregnant wife home. I'll be fine." Before he could keep the argument going, I turned away and headed up the street, my heels clacking against the frozen sidewalk.

Vanessa's voice was audible from behind me. "Let her be, Griffin. Take me home."

His door shut a moment later, and they were gone.

I felt perfectly safe in this city because I always stayed on the good side of town. I walked everywhere, and not once did I have a problem with anyone. If someone tried to mug me, I would just stab their dick with the heel of my boot.

I crossed two blocks then turned right to take a shortcut to the next street, a cobblestone alleyway next to a coffee shop. A couple of bicycles were leaning against the wall, and light chatter came from inside the fogged windows. I turned right and kept going.

That was when someone grabbed me.

One hand was flung across my mouth while the other gripped me around the waist. "She smells as good as she looks." A creepy voice spoke directly into my ear, the calmness of his tone more terrifying than the hand that silenced my mouth. He ripped off my jacket, leaving only my skintight dress behind.

"I find that hard to believe." A man emerged from

around the corner, dressed all in black with a beanie over his head. Approaching forty with a thick beard along his jaw, he looked like the devil spawn that roamed the streets late at night. He held a long piece of rope in his hands, which told me they didn't just want my clutch.

They wanted something else.

My survival instincts kicked in. I bit hard on his middle finger and bucked my hips at the same time.

"Bitch!" His hand loosened on my mouth as he jerked backward, his other arm releasing my waist.

I turned around and kicked him as hard as I could right between the legs.

"Fuck!" He gripped his balls and fell to the ground, so winded he couldn't even move.

I spat on him—just because he deserved it. Then I reached down and pulled out the knife I noticed sticking out of his belt.

"Get her!" The guy with the beard moved in behind me just as two other guys joined the fight.

I got the knife and turned around. "Touch me and see what happens." I held the knife just the way my father taught me, my other hand held at the ready while the rest of my body maintained a defensive posture.

"Oh, I will touch you." He nodded to one of the other men, telling him to move in behind me.

I was surrounded and outnumbered, but I'd rather die than let them take me. I would fight my way out of this, never giving up.

I heard the sound of a cocking gun behind me. "Drop the knife, bitch."

I didn't turn around, keeping my eyes on the guy with the beard and the rope. "Stop calling me bitch. You three are the ones acting like bitches." I turned around, my knife still held at the ready. I came face-to-face with the black gun pointed at my face.

I kept a neutral expression, but I was terrified. A barrel was pointed directly between my eyes, and my life depended on the finger squeezing the trigger. Just ten minutes ago, I was dining with my family, getting fat off bread, and having a great time. Now I was fighting for my life, unsure what to do and how to survive.

But I wasn't gonna let these men take me. They didn't want my shit. My clutch was on the ground, and they could have snatched it and taken off by now. No, they wanted me—and that was something I would never give.

"Drop the knife, *bitch*." He took a step closer to me, the gun shaking in his hand.

Like the rest of the Barsettis, I was temperamental. Not to mention, insanely stubborn. "Don't. Call. Me. That." I threw the knife, hitting him right in the shoulder.

He immediately fell back, gripping his shoulder as the blade stuck out of the wound. "Jesus Christ!"

The man with the beard jumped on me and quickly wrapped my wrists in the rope. "Got her."

I used all my strength to push him off, but the rope was too tight.

He pushed me onto the ground, not caring that my dress had risen over my ass and now they could see my thong. "Damn, that's a fine ass."

I tried to kick him. "Let me go! Do you have any idea who I am?"

"Nope." The guy pulled out a piece of white fabric to bind my mouth. "But our dicks are about to find out."

"I'm Carmen Barsetti." My name was all I had. I came from a powerful and wealthy family, a group of men who would stop at nothing until they had me back. "And my father will butcher all of you."

"Shut up. We don't give a shit." He kicked me in the back.

The pain made me lurch forward, but I refused to cry out. "Well, you should. Because Bones is my brother."

That made them halt in their tracks. It turned quiet, and they all looked at each other because that name obviously meant something to them.

His name was my lifeline, so I kept using it. "And he won't stop until he gets me back. You know exactly what he'll do to all of you once he tracks me down. So let me go, and get the hell out of town."

They all looked at each other and seemed to come to an agreement. "If we let you go, we're as good as dead. That means we have to kill you when we're done—no tracks." The man shoved the fabric into my mouth and gagged me so all I could do was make muffled screams.

This couldn't be happening.

This couldn't be my ending.

My life had been so perfect just minutes before. Now I would be raped and killed.

My parents would never recover from it.

Carter would be haunted by it.

This death was a death to all the Barsettis.

"Let her go." A deep, masculine voice filtered through the alleyway, the baritone powerful and innately sexy. Full of authority and a hint of fearlessness, it was the voice of a man who wore an invisible crown.

The men turned silent, their shuffles absent because none of them was moving.

It was so quiet, I could hear the man's footsteps.

The men were still frozen in place.

I couldn't see the man because I was facing the other way. All I had to go off was the sound of his voice, the way it was rough like sandpaper but hard like steel. He sounded young, maybe a few years older than me. It wasn't Bones or one of my family members to save me. This man was a complete stranger—and he was provoking four armed men.

He spoke again. "Now."

The man with the beard released my wrists. "Bosco—"

"Not her." He snapped his fingers, commanding them like dogs. "Leave."

The rope was yanked off my wrists, and the gag was pulled out of my mouth. The only thing they left behind was my black clutch that had fallen to the ground at the beginning of the fight. Their footsteps were audible until they turned the corner in the alleyway and disappeared.

My dress was still yanked over my ass, so I stood up and pulled it down, reclaiming my dignity after it had been taken away. Even though I was safe now, I was more afraid of the man who'd saved me than those idiots. All he had to do was say a few words to get those men to leave. That was an absolute kind of power—and that scared me.

I knew I was safe from those monsters, but I wasn't stupid enough to think I was safe from him.

Once my dress was smoothed out, I faced the mysterious man named Bosco.

He was looking me up and down, checking me out without a hint of shame. His blue eyes started at my legs and slowly made their way up, following the curves of my figure until he settled on my face.

"Are you done?"

Amused, he gave a lopsided grin. "I'll never be done." He stepped closer to me, his black leather jacket tight on his thick arms. His muscles stretched the fabric, showing the physical representation of his strength underneath the clothing. He wore a black t-shirt underneath, and that was just as tight across his hard chest. He had narrow hips that led to dark jeans. He didn't seem to be armed—and that made his power even more impressive.

He stopped a few inches away from me, so tall that he had to bend his neck down to look at me. He still wore the same smile of amusement as he met my gaze.

When he shifted his eyes downward and looked down the top of my dress, his expression turned serious once more. "They made a good choice." With stubble across his hard jaw and blue eyes like Griffin's, he was a handsome man who didn't belong in a dark alleyway. He belonged on a billboard or in a magazine. He didn't need to kidnap a woman when he could sink himself into any pussy he wanted.

Like every other woman in the world, I wasn't immune to his charms. He was a panty-soaker, a man I would take home in a heartbeat. Even if he told me he was a playboy who would be gone the second he was finished, that would have been fine with me—because he would make me come.

I didn't like his arrogance, the way he thought he owned me just because he chased away those assholes. Without knowing a single thing about him, I knew he was from the underworld. He was the biggest predator in the food chain, the great white in the ocean. I didn't underestimate his power, but I didn't get on my knees and thank him either. "What do you want?"

He cocked his head slightly, his amusement increasing. "What makes you think I want anything?"

"Because you're worse than they are."

His eyes narrowed, and he stared at me for several heartbeats. He held my gaze without blinking, absorbing my words well after I'd said them. Long stretches of silence didn't affect him at all. He seemed to thrive on it. "You're a smart woman."

My heart started to beat harder. I considered crying for help, but I suspected he would rip out my throat before I got the chance. His killer good looks didn't mask the dangerous undertone he possessed. I'd been around powerful men long enough to recognize it from a mile away. He had the same aura as Griffin, the sort of man that could be equally evil or kind depending on the mood he was in. "What do you want?" Did he want to drug me and throw me in the back of a van? Or did he want me to get on my knees and suck him off as a thank you? It didn't matter—he wasn't getting either.

"I didn't want anything until I got a good look at you —and that mouth of yours." His eyes flicked down to my lips, and he stared at them for a while, his own jaw hardening with desire.

A shiver moved down my spine. I was both aroused and terrified at the exact same time.

"I don't do this often."

"What?" I whispered.

"Save a damsel in distress. Normally, I just keep walking."

"I'm not a damsel," I shot back.

"But you were certainly in distress until I came along." He took a step closer to me, bringing us in together until our mouths were practically touching. "Or would you rather me hand you back over?"

This man was certainly more dangerous, but I preferred his company over the others. I didn't like him, but I was still affected by his sheer magnitude, his gravitational pull that rivaled the sun. "If you think I'm gonna suck your dick as a thank you, you're wrong. I would rather fight my way to freedom than submit to any man." My pride would get me killed someday, but I would rather die with honor than submit out of fear. As a Barsetti, I held my head high and bowed to no one.

That slight look of amusement was there again. He stared into my face like he was transfixed, mesmerized by the backtalk coming out of my mouth. "You know how to make a man hard, sweetheart."

"Don't call me sweetheart."

He sucked a breath in between his teeth again, like my mouth was only making him want me more. "Carmen." He said the name slowly, feeling it across his tongue as if he were tasting it.

I hadn't told him my name, which meant he'd been listening to the confrontation for minutes before he intervened. Why did he wait so long? Did he consider walking by and ignoring it?

"I didn't want anything in exchange for saving you. But I changed my mind."

"You aren't getting anything." Somebody else would be thanking him from the bottom of her heart, but I wasn't that stupid. I knew this guy was bad news.

"I want that smartass mouth on mine. I want a kiss, the kind packed with as much fire and spunk as your words. Give it to me, and I'll let you go."

After all that, he just wanted a kiss?

He kept watching me, waiting for me to give my answer.

"A man should save a woman because it's the right thing to do."

"I'm not a man—I'm a monster." He said it casually, like he was even proud of it. "As I said, I don't do this. I normally would have walked by and ignored this confrontation in a heartbeat. I don't give a shit about a stupid woman who walks home alone at night. If you were smarter, you wouldn't be in this situation."

"A woman should have the right to walk wherever she wants, whenever the hell she wants. Don't blame this attack on me. Blame the assholes who wanted to rape me. They're the problem, not me."

"Spin it however you want, sweetheart," he said coldly. "That's the world we live in—and you know it. As a Barsetti, you know better. Imagine the disappointment of your father if he knew."

"Don't talk about my family." This man didn't know anything about me, and I wouldn't let him bring my father into the mix. "If you don't care about saving an innocent woman, why did you save me?"

His broad shoulders looked muscular in his jacket, and the thick stubble on his face matched the nighttime shadows. It was cold that night, but there was so much adrenaline in my bloodstream that I'd forgotten about it until now. Now that I could see the vapor coming out of his nostrils as he breathed, I remembered it was a freezing night in winter. I was still standing in a small piece of fabric, this man growling at me like a hungry wolf. "Bones is your brother?"

My family name hadn't meant anything to those men, but Bones's certainly did. A ruthless hitman who wasn't afraid of anything, his reputation acted as a personal security blanket around me. Maybe my fate would have been completely different if I'd never mentioned him. "Brother-in-law."

He nodded slightly, like that was the information he was looking for. "I owe him a favor. My debt is repaid."

Now I was truly afraid. I'd just stepped into the underworld, and the reality was cutting off my air supply. I could barely breathe because there just wasn't enough oxygen in the air. If this man knew Bones, that meant their characters must be the same. He could be a killer, a rapist, anything...and I was alone with him.

"But I still want that kiss."

My breathing had increased because I couldn't hide my physical needs. Unfortunately, the vapor rose out of my mouth at a quicker rate, showing him just how nervous I'd become. "And if I say no?"

He moved closer to me and placed his warm finger-tips against the back of my frozen neck. He gripped me gently, his fingers reaching under the fall of my hair. He didn't kiss me, but he invaded my space, his cologne and body soap mixing together and forming a tantalizing aroma. It was the scent of pure masculinity, of a man with so much power in his touch alone. "You won't." His eyes flicked down to my mouth as he held me in place, his stubble so close to my lips. His arm moved around my waist with a powerful hold. He tugged on me slightly, arching the curve in my back and bringing me closer into his chest.

He was so warm, and his grip was so strong. Like probably every other woman, I'd fallen prey to his touch. The context of our interaction didn't seem to matter because my attraction outweighed everything else. Reduced to a biological need, all I wanted was that kiss he demanded from me. It was more than a fair trade after what he did for me, but I found myself wanting to kiss him...just because.

"Say yes." His thumb rested against my jawline, and he angled my neck back more, gaining better access to my mouth with our differences in height. He was over six feet, making me over a foot shorter than him. His thumb brushed across my cheek, and he practically breathed into my mouth as he waited.

For a man who could do whatever he wanted, it was odd that he was waiting for permission. Maybe it was Bones's presence still protecting me. Maybe that made me invincible. "Yes."

The second he heard that word, his mouth was on mine. He came in aggressively, but his kiss was surprisingly soft. He touched my mouth with purposeful pulls, really feeling my lips as he breathed into me. His arm tightened around my waist, and he pulled me closer into him.

Making me feel the stiff outline in his jeans.

Jesus.

He turned his head to the right, positioning my mouth for a deeper angle. Like a man deeply in love, he worshiped my mouth with passion, moving his lips with mine at the perfect speed and intensity. It wasn't sloppy, and it wasn't slow either. He kept me on my toes, enjoying me like this was the sexiest kiss he'd ever experienced.

It certainly was mine.

He cradled the back of my head as he gave me his tongue. With a quick swipe against mine along with a warm breath, he protected me from the cold and made me melt right at his feet.

Now I was lost.

I felt his hard chest as I moved my hand up his t-shirt, touching the muscles that were as hard as a slab of concrete. My fingers felt the cord in his neck as I made my way to his short brown hair. I fisted the strands in my fingertips, and I matched his passion with my own. He was a monster, a man of the underworld, but that didn't change the way my body responded to him. Good or evil, I wanted him.

My hand touched his jawline next, the thick stubble coarse against my fingertips. My thumb brushed across his bottom lip as I kissed him. Every single inch of him was all man, especially the enormous hard-on pressed right against my stomach. If I could measure him with my fingers, he had to be at least nine inches. On top of that, he was thick.

Monster cock.

He turned my hips and guided me to the wall of the alley. Our kisses turned from a smolder to raging fire. He pressed my back against the freezing stone and sank into me, covering me with his entire body as he continued to claim my mouth. He sucked my bottom lip into his mouth before he released it. "This." He kissed my top lip this time, breathing against my mouth as he looked me in the eye. "Mouth." He dug his hand into my hair again as he kissed me harder.

I didn't care that we were in the middle of a dark alley and my panties were getting wetter by the second. I didn't care if this man was a murderer or a thief. All I cared about was keeping his mouth on mine, making this kiss last forever. I'd had good sex and hot kisses, but nothing like this. This was the first time I'd ever come this close to the sun. I was about to get burned, but I didn't care.

He grabbed my left leg and hiked it over his hip, pressing me farther into the wall so his cock hit right against my clit.

God.

He gripped the back of my thigh and kept my leg in place as he started to grind against me, rubbing his thick length right against my throbbing clit. Without breaking the kiss, he dry-humped me right there in the dark alleyway, right there in the middle of winter.

And I wanted him to.

My nails clawed at him harder, and my mouth ached

for more of his. Our tongues danced together, we breathed as one, and I gripped the front of his t-shirt because I was eager for him to take it off.

My hand slid up under his shirt, and that's when I touched the rock-hard abs that felt like mountains. My fingers slid along the deep grooves as they made their way up to his hard chest. My thumb flicked over his nipple then stroked his pecs.

What a beautiful man.

He kept grinding against me, his huge cock hitting my clit in just the right spot.

Fuck, he was gonna make me come. Right in the middle of this ice-cold alleyway where I'd just been assaulted. I didn't know anything about him besides his name, but my hips were rocking with his, and I couldn't stop picturing how that dick would feel inside me.

He gave me his tongue again, and that's when I came.

"Fuck...yes." I gripped his shoulder and moaned in his mouth, my hips bucking against him as an awesome climax overcame me.

He stopped kissing me—just so he could stare at me. With hard eyes that burned with desire, he watched me convulse against his cock, his arrogance at its peak. His jaw was clenched hard as his fingers dug into the back of my thigh.

Watching him enjoy my climax just made me come harder. I moaned in the alleyway for an orgasm that was better than any I'd had during intercourse—or with my hand. My panties were soaked and I knew they were smearing against his jeans, but my mind was so far in the clouds that I didn't care.

He kissed me again when I finished, a smile on his lips.

That orgasm felt so good that I didn't care about being embarrassed. I wanted to keep my dignity, even now. My head rested against the cold wall, and I stared into his handsome face, his throbbing cock still pressed against my pussy.

"That was one hell of a kiss." His hand was still in my hair, and he grinned like he'd just been crowned as king.

"Wasn't bad." I dropped my leg and adjusted my dress. Like I'd expected, there was a dark spot on his jeans—a pussy stain I couldn't erase.

He glanced at it then looked at me, his arrogance at an all-time high. "Yeah...not bad."

I moved around him, keeping my head high and my back straight. My clutch was still on the ground and so was my jacket. I pulled on my coat and buttoned it up, hiding my curves from view as I retrieved my purse.

He came up behind me, his heavy footsteps audible in the silence.

I adjusted my hair then turned to face him. "Good night, Bosco."

He stared at me with those cryptic blue eyes, his thoughts a mystery behind that stone-cold gaze. His hands moved into the pockets of his jeans, and his hard cock still made the front of his jeans rise with a bulge. "I like the way you say my name."

He probably expected me to invite him over for the
night. If he made every woman come like that, then he
was probably used to women begging for him. I should
be no different, but I refused to let that happen. I didn't
know much about this man, but I knew he was bad news.
He might be beautiful as hell, but he was also dangerous
as hell. I'd gotten a climax that would put me to sleep the
second I got home. When I woke up in the morning, I
would forget about this man forever. "You'll never hear
me say it again."

2

BOSCO

I stood at the window of my apartment, on the top floor of the building I owned, and looked down at the city. It was the middle of the night, hours after Carmen had walked away from me in the alleyway. She'd pulled on her coat, flipped her hair, and left without giving me a backward glance.

Hot as hell.

I expected her to ask to see me again after she soaked my jeans with her arousal. But as if I meant nothing to her, she forgot about me the second I was out of her sight.

Made me want her more.

Carmen Barsetti...what an interesting woman.

She'd just been assaulted by four men, a gun pointed to her head with rope wound around her wrists. On her knees in an alleyway, her end seemed imminent. But she got to her feet again and carried on like nothing happened.

And she fought every step of the way. She stabbed a knife in one guy's shoulder and broke the balls of another. There wasn't a hint of tears in her eyes, not a sign of a plea for mercy.

She fought like a man.

I'd never come across a woman like her.

Fearless.

I pulled my phone out of my pocket and made the call.

It only rang twice before he answered, a deep voice packed with annoyance. "It's three in the morning. What the fuck do you want?" Bones practically growled over the line, a bear that had been stirred from hibernation. He was easily provoked, a temper that soared and never came down again.

"I wouldn't call unless it was important."

"What's important to you isn't important to me." The background around him was silent. He was probably at his apartment in Milan, staring at a different skyline than I was now. "I've retired, Bosco. Whatever you're about to ask me for, just assume my answer is no."

I didn't know he was out of the game. He seemed too young to hang up his badge as the greatest hitman in western Europe. "Congratulations. What are you doing these days? Fishing?" I couldn't picture a man like Bones doing nothing. It didn't seem possible.

"I'm married."

"You retired to get married?" I asked. "Sounds boring."

"Marry the right woman, and it'll never be boring. So what the hell do you want?"

I didn't ask him any more questions, knowing he wouldn't give me answers. "I don't want anything. I wanted you to know that we're even."

"Even, huh? How so?"

"I ran into your sister-in-law tonight."

He was dead silent.

"Carmen, right?"

He turned even more sinister, like I'd just hit one of his buttons. "What about her?"

"She was walking home alone. A few guys snatched her in an alleyway. I happened to be walking by, but since this isn't my scene, I wasn't going to intervene. But then she dropped your name as a last attempt to save herself...so I had to do something. I scared the guys off and got her out of there." I skipped the part about the make-out session against the wall, along with the pussy juice she left on my jeans. "So, I think that makes us even."

Bones was quiet on the line, obviously battling the rage that pounded in his temples. His relief at her safety was nothing compared to his anger that she had been in danger in the first place. "Tell me who they are."

"You know I can't do that, man. I've got a reputation to uphold."

"Bosco—"

"I can't." As the king of this city, I couldn't be a rat. I was a villain, not a hero. Money would only keep flowing in if my reputation was impeccable. Secrecy was a big deal in my line of work. It gave me all the power—because I knew everything. Men only came to my club because they knew they were untouchable under my reign. "I know you want revenge, but I can't. I won't say it again."

Bones knew I was as stubborn as he was, so he didn't push. "She's alright?"

"Yes. Not the least bit shaken up—at least not in front of me."

"She's not the kind of woman to show weakness."

"Yeah...I noticed."

"Stay away from her, Bosco."

When I grinned, I saw my reflection in the floor-to-ceiling glass. "I saved her, didn't I?"

"I mean it," he threatened. "I'm not blind to the way men look at her. I see her as a sister, but our familial relationship doesn't change the fact that she's absolutely stunning. I know what a guy like you is thinking when you're near her. She's off-limits."

"You know I don't chase pussy. It chases me."

"She's not pussy," he said with a growl. "Talk about her like that again, and I'll kill you."

"Wasn't referring to her specifically. You know what I mean. And when am I going to get a thank you?"

He was quiet again, his anger clearly smoldering.

"You said we're even, so you won't get any gratitude from me."

That's what I thought he would say. "Fair enough. Tell the wife I said hi."

He hung up.

I shoved the phone into my pocket and continued to stare at the city skyline. The lights stopped at the edge, the rest of Tuscany quiet in the background. The second I came home, I should have dropped my jeans and put my hand to work around my cock, but that didn't sound appealing. After I'd had those luscious lips against mine, I wanted to have them again. I wanted the real thing, to feel that desire between her legs against my skin, not through my jeans.

As I'd said, I didn't chase pussy. Not my style. There was no woman out there worth that kind of effort.

But then again, there was no woman like Carmen Barsetti.

THE BASEMENT OF MY BUILDING WAS USED FOR ONE purpose only.

The Brawl.

Men were gathered in a circle around the ring, ready to get the bets started. I made my billions operating the largest underground casino in all of Europe. The cops knew about it, but they never crossed me because I was an opponent who couldn't be defeated. Besides, when I was handing out Christmas bonuses that matched their yearly salary, it was easy for them to turn the other way.

Jones escorted the first asshole into the ring and unlocked his cuffs. Shirtless and in jeans, he was a man in his late thirties with an entire sleeve of tattoos on his left arm. His hair had been shaved as a requirement, and he'd been locked up for three days prior to now—without being able to say his goodbyes.

The next man was pushed into the ring, about a decade older, out of shape. It didn't seem like he had a chance.

The crowd started making their bets.

"Alright." I stepped into the circle, my arms crossed over my chest as the men around me immediately turned silent. "Both of you assholes crossed the casino, which means you crossed me. Cheating and stealing are fatal offenses. But since I'm a merciful guy...I'll give each of you a chance. You'll fight to the death. Winner gets to live—and tell the tale of his punishment." I clapped my hands twice. "Good luck, gentlemen." The second I stepped out of the ring, the fight began.

And I watched the blood run.

3

CARMEN

My crazy night turned into a strange blur. The details of the attack seemed to lose relevance, like they weren't nearly as important as what happened afterward. Bosco pushed me against a wall, ground against me until I came, and gave me a kiss I would never forget.

I kept replaying it in my mind the next day at work. I made a few arrangements, but since I was so distracted, I made double the arrangements I needed and wasted the flowers. I put them in the window in the hope someone would buy them.

I didn't want to see Bosco again. That guy was bad news.

But why couldn't other men kiss like that?

Why couldn't other men have confidence like that?

I'd never met a man quite like him. I'd never seen anyone so damn beautiful. That jawline alone was worth a million dollars. His eyes were like diamonds, and his body was hard as concrete. He'd probably picked up a woman after we went our separate ways and fucked her in his bed—but picturing that only turned me on.

Because I wanted to be the woman in his bed.

A part of me wanted to ask Griffin about him, to see exactly how dangerous he was. Griffin used to be a hitman, but he'd never been a danger to my family. Maybe Bosco's crimes were petty.

But I had a feeling they weren't.

The bell rang overhead as the door opened and a customer stepped inside.

"Good afternoon." I looked up from my arrangement. "How may I—" The words died in my throat when I saw Griffin staring me down like he might rip my head off. His eyes looked like bullets, and I was his target. Judging by the look on his face, he knew everything that happened last night.

Everything.

Shit.

He locked the door behind him and approached the counter, no longer the protective and concerned older brother I viewed him as. When Vanessa first started seeing him, I couldn't deny that I thought he was sexy as hell. But that attraction died away soon after that, knowing he was meant for someone else. Now he seemed like a brother, a more intense version of Carter. Griffin gripped the edge of the counter with both hands and looked down at me, disappointment and rage in his eyes.

This should be fine. "Alright...I'll get a ride next time."

He slammed his right hand onto the counter as hard as he could. "Shut the fuck up, Carmen."

My eyes almost popped out of my head because they snapped open so quickly. "Excuse me—"

"I've always respected you since the day we met. But that respect is gone now because you didn't listen to me. You're arrogant, and your arrogance almost got you killed last night. I admire you for being a strong woman like Vanessa, but I don't admire you for being stupid—"

"Listen—"

"No, you listen." He slammed his fist again. "You were careless, and we both know it. When you're the kind of woman that looks the way you do, you always have to be careful. Men will never stop wanting you, and if they see you alone, they'll hunt you."

I shut my mouth, knowing Griffin was too angry to be reasoned with.

"You have money, so there's no reason not to take a taxi."

"It was two blocks away—"

His eyes looked like grenades.

"Alright, alright. I'll always take a taxi from now on."

That wasn't enough for Griffin. He was still pissed. "I don't need to tell you how that could have ended."

"I know." I would be lying if I said I hadn't been scared. I had been terrified. When those ropes were bound around my wrists and that gun was pointed in my face, I thought that was the end. I thought about how devastated my parents would be if they lost their only daughter.

"And if Bosco hadn't owed me a favor, you might be dead right now."

"I know, Griffin."

When he saw the remorse on my face, he finally simmered down to a gentle boil. "I'm not worried about you just for Vanessa. I'm worried about you because I care about you. If something bad happened to you, it would hurt me." He placed his hand over his heart. "You're family to me, Carmen."

"I know," I whispered.

"Then you need to learn from this. Learn from your mistake."

"Trust me, I already have." I knew I had no right to ask him for anything, not after I'd made him so angry, but I had to try. "Please don't tell my father."

He bowed his head and sighed.

"Please. It'll just get him worked up, and I don't want to do that."

"I don't know..."

"I'm not in danger, so there's nothing to tell him. You're just going to upset him."

He considered my request before he lifted his gaze and looked at me. "I'll make an arrangement with you. Never let that shit happen again, and we have a deal. You let me walk you home, or you get a ride. Alright?"

"Deal."

"Promise me?" he pressed.

"Yes...I promise."

He finally leaned back, his ripped muscles less tense now that the conversation was over.

"You saved my life, Griffin." The Barsetti name wasn't enough to spare me. It was only when I dropped his name that I got mercy. What would have happened if I didn't have that weapon in my arsenal? "Thank you."

"I didn't do anything," he said quietly.

"But just your reputation spared me..."

"That's not true either. Bosco owed me a favor. If he hadn't, he would have ignored you."

I wanted to know more about this mysterious man. Bosco said he was a monster, not a man. He said he was evil and didn't flinch as he said it. But what kind of evil were we talking about? "Who is he?"

"Bosco?" he asked.

"Yeah. He scared off four guys...just by saying a few words." He had immense power without having to enforce it. He was a strong man, clearly muscular but not beefy the way Griffin was. Every part of his body was hard like steel, even his dick. "He didn't even have a gun." The only reason why I knew that was because his body was crushed against mine and I didn't feel it anywhere.

"Doesn't surprise me. He's the king of the city."

"The king?"

"He controls all the money."

I wasn't following this. "What? What are you talking about?"

"It doesn't matter, Carmen. He's just like me—lethal. He's one of the biggest criminals in this city, in all of Europe. He's not someone you should interact with for any reason whatsoever. I told him to stay away from you. But if you see him, tell me immediately."

"Did he say he wanted to see me again?"

"No. Why?"

It was becoming obvious Griffin had no idea about our kiss. "You warned him to stay away from me... Why would you do that?"

"Come on, Carmen." He didn't roll his eyes, but it seemed like he wanted to. "Look at you. He eats women like you for lunch."

I knew Bosco was a playboy—that much was obvious. "Does he...traffic women or anything like that?"

"No. He's not that kind of criminal."

That was a relief.

"I just don't want him to think you're one of his girls. That's all."

"One of his girls?"

"Yeah. A man like him is used to getting whatever he wants."

I already knew all that information, but hearing it out loud still disappointed me. Bosco wasn't just a bad boy, but the kind of man that would ruin your life. It was smart for me to walk away without looking back. I would never see him again, and that was exactly how it should be. His kiss would be my favorite of all time, but that could just be a memory for me to look back on when I touched myself.

"Why are you asking all these questions?"

Griffin's voice brought me back to the conversation, and I feared I was making my interest obvious. "He saved my life. I'm just curious."

"I hope that's all, Carmen. Because he's not good enough for you."

"You say that about every guy..."

"Because it's true. There're no men in the world good enough for Barsetti women."

"What about you?" I countered, referring to Vanessa.

He held my gaze for a long time, not blinking. "I'm no exception."

AFTER A WEEK PASSED, THE MEMORY OF THAT NIGHT started to fade from my mind.

As did the memory of Bosco.

I had a date on Saturday night with one of the guys who came into the shop to buy his mother flowers for her birthday. He seemed nice enough. He didn't have the sexy confidence I liked in Bosco, and he didn't possess a silent power I found intimidating, but that shouldn't matter. I wasn't looking for a criminal.

Just a normal guy.

The flower shop was slow that day. People usually picked up their arrangements closer to the weekend. The only time I worked during the week was for funerals. Weddings and bridal showers always took place on Saturdays and Sundays.

The bell rang overhead when a customer came into the shop. My back was to the door as I stood at the table, tying a ribbon around a vase. My shears were on the table along with chopped rose stems. My gloves were thick to protect my fingers from the thorns—a gift my father got me for my birthday a few years ago.

Heavy footfalls sounded behind me, the long gait sounding like the stride of a tall man. I set the scissors down and turned around. "Good afternoon. How can I —" Words died in my throat when my eyes locked on to the beautiful blue ones that had watched me come just a week ago. My entire body stiffened at his unexpected visit, especially since he looked even more handsome than he did last week. Today, he'd ditched the jacket and wore a black t-shirt, his forearms chiseled with thick cords of muscle. His skin was tanned, just a few shades darker than mine. A shiny watch was on his wrist, but that was the only jewelry he wore. His fitted jeans hung low on his hips, tight around his muscled thighs.

He wore that same lopsided grin he'd had when he first looked at me. "You know your way around those scissors." He slid his hands into his pockets, his confidence filling the room just the way it filled the alleyway. He stepped to the side to examine the flower arrangement I'd just made. His blue eyes took in the flowers and the vase before he turned back to me. "Nice."

I forced myself to recover from his unexpected visit. I was usually more confident than this, even when I was nervous. "Picking up some flowers for your girlfriend?"

He grinned at my joke. "For my mother, actually."

I forced my eyes not to soften. Just because he was a criminal didn't mean I should be touched by his gesture —especially if he was lying. "What does she like?" Instead of asking why he was really there and letting him see my anxiety, I acted indifferent. The last thing I wanted was for him to think he got under my skin.

"Anything." He walked to the fridge and pulled out an arrangement wrapped in plastic. "This will do."

"You don't want it in a vase?" I asked, knowing that made flowers look a lot more elegant.

"No." He carried the flowers back to the counter and set them on the surface. "Vases don't belong in a cemetery."

I froze at his statement, my heart immediately moving into my throat. I loved my mother so much, and I would be devastated if I ever lost her. Knowing he'd lost someone he loved, even if he wasn't a good man, broke my heart. "I'm so sorry..."

Bosco watched my expression, his eyes showing the same hardness they did before. "I can read people really well. I can tell you mean that."

"Of course I do." I wrapped his flowers in extra paper then grabbed my iPad. "Fifteen euros."

He pulled out his wallet then set the cash on the table. "Thank you." He grabbed the flowers and held them in the crook of his arm. There was nothing left to discuss now that he'd finished his purchase, but he continued to linger, his eyes glued to my face like my lips were a piece of artwork.

I knew he was thinking about our kiss—because I was.

I refused to break eye contact, to show any kind of weakness. When faced with a bigger and stronger opponent, you had to rise to the challenge—otherwise, they would walk all over you. If he could see through my front, that wouldn't matter. I still had to try. At least my enemies would respect me. "Have a good day, Bosco."

An unstoppable grin spread across his face, like every little thing I did was amusing. "I like you."

The compliment spread through my veins and made my skin feel warm. His approval should mean nothing to me, not when he was an underground criminal. So far, he didn't seem to be dangerous. If he'd really wanted to hurt me, he wouldn't have let me walk away from him that night. He wouldn't be surprising me in broad daylight at my shop. "Bones told you to stay away from me."

His grin slowly disappeared, his stunning blue eyes shifting to a menacing stare. "Do you want me to stay away from you?"

I should immediately say yes, but I didn't. I kept my silence and stared him down, unsure what to say in rebuttal. This was a guy I didn't want to get involved with, no matter how good that kiss was. I didn't mind an occasional bad boy here and there, nothing I couldn't handle. But Bosco was a whole new caliber, someone Bones was vehemently opposed to. I deflected the question by not answering it at all. "I would listen to Bones if I were you."

"I'm not afraid of him." He moved the flowers back onto the counter without breaking eye contact with me.

"You should be."

The corner of his mouth rose in a smile. "I'm the one he should be afraid of."

The warmth I felt a moment ago quickly disappeared. An ice-cold feeling replaced it, freezing my veins instantly. Those men stopped in their tracks the second I mentioned Bones's name. It was a name people instinctively feared, a name that protected Vanessa when she was taken by those thugs. But Bosco seemed genuinely indifferent to Griffin's power.

"I'm an opponent he can't outmatch—and he knows it." He spoke so confidently, so eloquently that he couldn't be lying. "Especially now that he's got a wife to think about."

Bones didn't specifically say why Bosco was so dangerous, but he'd definitely emphasized his authority.

"I owed him a favor, and I repaid it. Now, I don't owe him a damn thing." He leaned against the counter slightly, his head tilted to the side as he stared at me. Unnaturally suave, he was hypnotizing to watch. Men were rarely as self-assured as this guy. They called him the king of this city for a reason—because he controlled all the money. And if you controlled all the money, you controlled everyone. "Call him. See what happens." If it was a bluff, it was a damn good one.

That would be my first impulse, but since Bosco was far more intimidating than I realized, I found myself wanting to protect Bones rather than myself. "What do you want, Bosco?" My heart warned me with every beat. This guy was nowhere near average. He had more power than I could ever imagine. I'd dealt with sleazy guys who didn't understand the word no. I'd slapped a few men for grabbing my ass when I walked by. But those men were nothing compared to him.

"These beautiful flowers."

"Now that you have them, you should go." I held my ground the way every Barsetti should. We were innately proud, even if it cost us our lives in the process.

As if he didn't hear what I said, he kept staring at me.

I stared back, standing in my brown boots that zipped over my dark jeans. I wore a long-sleeved red sweater to fight the chill that came into the shop every time the door opened. At this time of year, the prices of flowers went up, but customers still stopped by.

He righted himself then grabbed the flowers off the counter. "Have dinner with me on Saturday night."

Now I knew without a doubt his appearance wasn't coincidental. He'd figured out I worked here and purposely stopped by. Who knew if those flowers were really for his mother. "I have a date."

His eyebrow rose slightly at my answer, and he was clearly irritated by that response.

"And even if I didn't, I'm not interested."

"Really?" He stepped closer to me, making me suck in a breath at his movement. "It seemed like you were interested last week."

"I was interested in my freedom. That's all."

That playful grin returned. "Sure. Whatever you say, sweetheart. I still have that stain on my jeans."

I refused to show my embarrassment even though I was mortified.

"And I still have the memory of that orgasm I gave you."

It was becoming harder to hold his gaze, more difficult to keep up this indifferent persona. When he was this close to me, I could smell the cologne and soap again. I could feel his lips without them touching me. I could feel the memory of that kiss wash over me like the waves of the ocean.

He moved even closer, until our faces were practically touching. His pretty blue eyes were even more brilliant when they were this close. For a man so dark, it seemed unnatural for him to be so beautiful.

I stopped breathing altogether, my entire body tensing at the way his proximity made me feel. My muscles tightened, and shivers ran up my spine. All I had to do was take a step back, but I didn't. I tilted my chin slightly so I could look up at him, angling my neck back so I could stare at the tall man looking down at me.

Like he had every right, he circled his arm around my waist, right into the steep curve of my back, and held me against him. His fingers clenched the fabric of my sweater at my side, making it stretch over my body even more.

I still hadn't taken a breath.

He leaned in and pressed his forehead to mine, his eyes shifting down to look at my body below him.

I wasn't sure how I'd gotten into this position, why I allowed him to touch me like this. My body was naturally attracted to his, from his pretty eyes to his muscular frame. My lips remembered exactly how that kiss felt, and I wanted another round. But my mind was still strong enough to fight it. "I want you to leave."

He sighed against me, his disappointment audible. "Why don't I believe you, sweetheart?" He pulled his head back and looked me in the eye, that same desire in his eyes that was there the other night. Then he cupped my cheek with his large palm and pressed a kiss to my lips. It was soft, not aggressive like the last one we shared. He moved his lips gently with mine, coaxing me into kissing him back. With a breath of air into my lungs, he brought my body to life once more.

Then he pulled away, ending the short kiss much sooner than the last. He dropped his hand from around my waist and grabbed the flowers off the counter. After a final heated look, he walked out of the flower shop and headed down the street.

My eyes followed him until he was no longer visible from the windows.

My fingertips immediately moved to my mouth, feeling the ache in my lips from the way he'd just kissed me. I could have been more persistent when I'd asked him to leave. But instead, I turned into all the other women who were obsessed with him. I kissed him back when he kissed me—and I enjoyed every second of it.

I had a feeling I would see him again.

———

SAMUEL WORKED FOR AN INSURANCE COMPANY. HE STARTED right at eighteen and slowly moved his way up in the company until he became the operations manager of his branch. He dealt with car insurance, along with home and life insurance. He told me a lot of details about his job that I didn't ask for, and that made the conversation last forever.

He was decently handsome and had a boyish smile that made him inherently charming. He didn't seem to ask me much about my life and only talked at length when he discussed himself. His eyes wandered over my body throughout dinner, making it obvious that he was staring at my tits.

Bosco did the same thing, but it wasn't creepy when he did it.

Samuel just couldn't pull it off.

Overall, it was one of the most boring dates I'd ever

had. He'd seemed a lot more charming at the flower shop when he was picking out an arrangement for his mom. But now that we were actually having a conversation, I was trying not to fall asleep.

And dream about the panty-soaker.

I squeezed my thighs together when I thought about that last kiss we'd had in the flower shop. It was short but sweet. If a simple kiss like that could make me wet, what would happen if we were both naked in my bed? The sweat would coat his thick muscles, and my hands would slide down all the intricate grooves of his body. His fat cock would fit inside me easily because I would be so damn wet.

"Carmen?" Samuel stared at me with concern on his face, like he'd just said something important.

"Sorry, what?" Thoughts of Bosco had made me drift away somewhere else. We sat in a quiet restaurant where some of the tables were occupied by other couples. We were right next to the window, the basket of bread untouched but our wineglasses empty. I knew this date wasn't going to go anywhere, so I was tempted to just walk out and forget it ever happened. Why was he wasting his time and mine?

"I asked if you were enjoying your food," he said, his voice quiet with disappointment. My disinterest was probably obvious to him.

"Oh," I said quickly. "Yes, it's great." I kept swirling my fork in the pasta without actually taking a bite.

"Well...it looks like you haven't eaten much of it."

"I'm just a slow eater." And it was hard to eat when I was thinking about screwing another guy.

His phone rang in his pocket, so he fished it out. "Sorry, I have to take this. You never know if it'll be a claim..."

"You're fine." I would rather sit quietly than keep talking to him anyway.

He put the phone against his ear. "This is Samuel." He turned quiet as he listened. His serious expression suddenly turned chalk-white, like he was listening to some terribly bad news. He didn't say a single word and continued to listen.

I couldn't hear the voice on the other line, so I had no idea what was going on.

Two men in black suits walked past our table and approached the other couples in the restaurant. One by one, the couples abandoned their tables along with the food and wine they were enjoying. They were escorted away in silence, the suits both muscular and intimidating.

There was definitely something wrong.

I looked out the window and saw a blacked-out car sitting at the curb. The windows were tinted pitch-black, and two more men in suits stood along the sidewalk, earpieces secured in their ears.

Oh shit.

Samuel finally said something into the phone. "Okay..." He hung up and put his phone in his pocket.

"Everything alright?"

Samuel didn't make eye contact with me again as he rose from the table. He didn't even push his chair in before he darted out of the restaurant, leaving his jacket behind.

Two men in suits immediately cleared the table, taking away the plates and glasses Samuel left behind. They placed a white candle in the center of the table alone with a new bottle of champagne. They poured two fresh glasses, and when the bottle was set on the table-cloth, I recognized the name.

It was a two-thousand-euro bottle of champagne.

Without any explanation, the men walked away.

I knew exactly who was behind this. Only one man in this city could clear out a restaurant and shut it down within two minutes. His guard escorted random patrons out of the restaurant without argument, which told me he paid them off just to keep them happy. I didn't have a clue what was said to Samuel, but judging by the paleness of his face, it was probably a threat.

I didn't try to leave because I knew Bosco's men would just push me back into the chair. With my legs crossed and my fingers wrapped around the expensive glass of champagne, I waited for the ruthless man to join me.

The back door to the car opened, and he emerged, over six feet of pure handsomeness. In a three-piece black suit with shiny shoes and a flashy watch, he looked like the rich man Bones rumored him to be. With hair perfectly styled and that damned lopsided grin, he looked right at me like this was some kind of game.

I faced forward and ignored him.

He entered the restaurant, and his footsteps sounded behind me. Heavy with a slow pace, he took his time as he approached my table. Before he even arrived, I could smell his scent, his pure masculinity that vibrated in the air around us.

He pulled out the chair and sat down, replacing Samuel like he'd never been there at all. His broad shoulders covered the chair behind him, and he made himself comfortable with his perfect posture. His hands rested in his lap, and he looked at me with an intense expression that mirrored the coldness of the Arctic. Twelve men took their places around the restaurant, securing each corner as well as the sidewalk outside. All armed and terrifying, they covered the perimeter with the effectiveness of an intelligence agency.

He didn't make a word of introduction before he sipped his wine.

"What are you doing here, Bosco?" Any other woman would be impressed with his stealthy entrance, but I refused to be. Any man who had bodyguards like that was someone I should stay away from. The fact that I was on his radar at all told me it was probably too late—I was already his prisoner.

"Our date. Remember?"

"Our date?" I asked, still surprised by his arrogance. "I said no."

"You must have misunderstood me, sweetheart. I never asked. I'm the kind of man that never asks." He brought his glass to his lips again and took another drink. Even that simple action was sexy. He licked his lips at the end, tasting every single drop of the bubbles and fruit blended together to provide a crisp and clean taste.

"That was pretty rude."

"Let's not pretend I didn't just rescue you from the most boring date of all time. It didn't seem like you were even listening to him most of the time. Now, that's pretty rude."

I shook my head slightly. "This asshole thing might work on the others, but it doesn't work on me."

"No, this asshole thing is just me. No stunt. And I think it does work on you. Not once did you try to leave."

"Like you would have let me."

"When have I ever *not* let you?" He cocked his head slightly, his eyes narrowing on me. "You've had every right to walk away whenever you want. To say no. To slap me even if you wanted to. But no, you want me as much as I want you."

"You're so arrogant."

"Maybe," he said with a shrug. "But I'm also right."

I rolled my eyes.

"Then leave." He challenged me with more than just his words. "Get up and walk out."

I kept my fingers resting against the stem of the glass, my eyes looking at the intimidating man across the table.

His suit fit him better than his own skin. The fabric hugged the muscles of his arms so perfectly. The cords in his neck were lickable. He'd shaved sometime that day because his jaw was completely clean. Somehow that made his eyes stand out even more.

"That's what I thought." He finished his glass then refilled it. "Let's cut the bullshit, sweetheart. You aren't the kind of woman that does something she doesn't want to do. So be a man about it—and say that you want me."

I stayed silent and refused to give him what he wanted. "Samuel may have been boring, but at least he was nice."

Bosco released a faint chuckle, like I'd made some kind of joke. "Sweetheart, I am being nice. Trust me…"

I glanced around once more at all the men who surrounded us. They were there for protection, but they made me uneasy. Why would a man need to be escorted to dinner like this? Just to spend time with a woman? "What now, Bosco?"

"We have dinner together." Without taking his eyes off me, he lifted his hand slightly and got the attention of one of his men. He ordered what he wanted then handed my plate to him. "Warm this up. Let's not waste food."

The man disappeared and left us alone again.

This was an interesting dining experience. "Is this how all your dates go?"

"No. I don't do dates."

"So I'm your first date?" I asked, slightly surprised.

"I guess so."

"No wonder why it's so strange." I drank from my glass, letting the insult sink in.

It didn't seem to affect him at all. "Why would you go out with a guy like Samuel in the first place?"

"He's nice."

"You don't want a nice guy. You want a guy who makes you come. Trust me, he doesn't fit the bill."

"You check out men often?" I teased.

He drank from his glass again. When he returned it to the table, he wore a slight smile. "I know how to read people. He's not your type."

"And what's my type?" I'd never had a serious relationship, so I really didn't know what I preferred.

He held my gaze for a long time, so confident that he could touch me with his presence without lifting a finger. "Me."

"You?" I asked incredulously. "The only things I ever hear about you are negative."

"Your point?"

Since he lived in a different reality, that probably didn't matter to him at all. A villain always thought he was a hero in his version of the story. "I don't want to get involved with a criminal."

"Yet, Bones is your brother-in-law."

"I didn't marry him."

"You still see him as family. At least, I know that's how he sees you. He's protective of you."

I knew Bones would do anything for me since Vanessa was his whole world.

"And I'm glad you didn't mention any of this to him —for his sake."

I was constantly teetering on the edge of hatred. Bosco's arrogance was suffocating, but the second he flashed that handsome smile, I wanted to kiss him again. I hated his menacing presence, but it didn't dull my attraction to him. "I don't need a man to defend me. I can take care of myself."

He took a drink of his wine and didn't say anything in response.

My legs were crossed under the table, and I squeezed my thighs together, attracted to that hard jawline of his. I wanted to sprinkle kisses across it, to feel those soft lips once more. But I also despised him at the same time. I'd never been more conflicted than I was now.

"The Barsettis are a well-respected family. Your uncle and father have quite a reputation."

"Which is why this dinner of yours is a stupid idea."

He propped both of his arms on the table, his hands resting right in the center. His watch reflected the light, and he leaned forward slightly, getting closer to me. "Regardless of what you think of my character, I don't enjoy mindlessly killing people. So if you want to protect your family, I would suggest you keep your mouth shut. I have no intention of hurting you, so you aren't in danger."

"Doesn't seem that way."

His eyes narrowed even farther, slightly terrifying. "If you were, you would know."

This man was an enigma. He seemed to be a criminal with morals.

"You can walk away from me at any time, as I've already said."

"You made me kiss you for my freedom."

He grinned. "Sweetheart, I would have let you walk away if you'd put up a better fight. But we both know you didn't want to put up a fight. Just like the last two times our lips touched, you want it to happen. You're trying to fight it, but I'm not sure why. I'm a decent guy if you get to know me."

"Bones told me to stay away from you."

"Of course he did. I don't disagree with that."

I grabbed the glass and took a long drink, depleting all the liquid and sending it into my stomach. "Then maybe I should listen to his advice."

He nodded behind me, indicating the exit. "There's the door." He kept calling my bluff, knowing I was attracted to him the second we kissed in that alleyway. We were both seduced by the same spell, unable to fight the epic passion our bodies ignited. "Tell me about yourself."

"I suspect you already know everything...considering you showed up to my work and my date."

"Tell me something that I wouldn't be able to figure out." He drank from his glass again, and just when he returned it to the table, the waiter arrived with our entrees. The plates were set in front of us, along with the new silverware and a fresh basket of bread. Bosco held my gaze the entire time, indifferent to everything going on around us.

When we were alone again, I spoke. "I want to fall in love and sleep beside the same man every single night for the rest of my life. I want four children and a place here in Florence, so I can walk to work every day. When I'm meant to meet that man, I will. In the meantime, I'm having fun until that moment arrives."

Bosco's face didn't show a hint of reaction to my statement. "Four kids?"

"Four."

"Wow. Ambitious."

"I'm up for the challenge."

He gave me a half smile in response. "You have the right hips for birthing babies—and making babies."

Every time he complimented me, my heart skipped a beat. He was transparent in his desire, and his masculinity made me feel deeply feminine. His narrow hips would fit perfectly between my thighs. His broad shoulders would cover my body as he lay on top of me, his weight sinking me deep into the sheets as he thrust inside me. "How many children do you want to have?"

The corner of his mouth rose in a smile. "You know how many."

I'd met guys like him before, smug and good-looking. They would never settle down until their beautiful looks started to fade and their promiscuity started to become pathetic. Bosco had nothing but symmetrical features, a perfect jawline, cheekbone structure, and eyes so cold they were actually hot. As he aged, he would probably be even better-looking, like a fine painting.

"Tell me about your flower shop."

"I've been running it for three years. I always knew I wanted to be a florist—and now I am."

"Impressive."

"It's not that impressive. My father bought the shop for me—but I'm paying him back."

"Not any different from getting a loan from a bank. Still impressive."

"My job doesn't feel like work. I create beautiful things all day long. I design arrangements for weddings and showers. I make the perfect display for funerals. It's very fulfilling. I hope I can do it for the rest of my life."

Unlike Samuel, Bosco seemed genuinely interested in what I was saying. His eyes were glued to mine as he listened, never straying to my chest or my hair. His gaze on my eyes, he listened attentively. "I'm sure you will."

"My cousin Vanessa owns her own gallery a few blocks away. It seems like we both inherited the creative gene."

"I agree."

"She's the one who married Bones."

"Which means he's your cousin-in-law, not your brother-in-law."

I shrugged. "Vanessa feels like a sister, and that's how I see her. And Bones treats me like a brother would, being protective even when I ask him not to be."

"You should be grateful you have someone like that

in your corner. A lot of women would give anything to feel protected like that."

That was one of the reasons Vanessa fell in love with him. She said she never felt safer than she did when she was with him. I never wanted him to walk me home because I wasn't his responsibility. "One day I'll meet a man for the job. But for now, I can handle myself."

He didn't tell me otherwise, even though he was the one who'd saved me. "I noticed you've been taking a taxi everywhere you go."

I wasn't surprised that he was spying on me, judging by the way he infiltrated the restaurant so easily.

"Smart."

"Bones requested it."

"You have a lot of respect for him."

"I do. But he's also family...and you do things for family."

He picked up his fork and started to eat, not having a reaction to my comment about family. He managed to keep his gaze on me as he ate, having control of everything in his vicinity.

My food was warm again and much more delicious than it'd been before. "What did you do with Samuel?"

"Told him I was your husband."

I almost spat out my food. "You did what?"

"And threatened to kill him if he ever came near you again." He said it nonchalantly, like it was no big deal.

"Wow. So you made me look like a cheater. And then

you threatened a man whose only crime was asking me out?"

"You didn't like him anyway, so what does it matter?" He took a break from his food and sipped his wine.

"I'm starting not to like you." I set my fork down and grabbed my clutch from the table. I liked a confident man, but I didn't like a controlling psychopath. "Good night, Bosco." I rose to my feet, the backs of my knees pushing the chair out.

Bosco was on his feet instantly. "Sweetheart—"

"One." I held up my forefinger. "A man doesn't call me sweetheart unless he's earned it. You definitely haven't earned it, Bosco." I held up a second finger. "Two. You said I could leave, and that's exactly what I'm doing."

He slowly slid his hands into his pockets, a quiet sigh sounding under his breath. His jaw tightened, the muscles in his cheek shifting slightly. Disappointment burned in his eyes as he fought the helpless feeling.

"Yes, I think you're hot. But I also think you're a psychopath who's overstepped his boundaries. I don't give a damn if you've got the entire city on your payroll and you can move mountains and claim restaurants. Your money and power don't impress me. I'm not like the women you're used to—stupid, submissive, and superficial. So don't waste another moment of your time on me —because I don't want it." I turned around and marched off, and to my relief, none of his men tried to stop me. I made the long walk to the front of the empty restaurant and finally out into the cool nighttime air. There was so much adrenaline in my veins that I didn't need my coat —even though it was my favorite.

I turned the corner and searched for a taxi, but the street was empty of cars. I didn't want to stand around and have Bosco stare at me through the window so I kept walking.

"Carmen." His powerful voice sounded behind me, echoing against the buildings even though he didn't raise his voice.

I should just keep walking, but for some idiotic reason, I stopped. I ground my teeth together in self-loathing as I stood in my boots, the freezing air hurting my lungs. I closed my eyes and willed myself to keep walking. Instead, I turned around.

He walked up to me and held out my black coat so I could put my arms through the sleeves. He wore the same disappointed expression, but his mouth was clenched tightly like he was stopping himself from saying anything else.

My heart softened at the gesture, and I hated myself for feeling any kind of empathy for him. But I loved that coat so much that I slid my arm into one sleeve and then the other.

Bosco pulled it over my shoulders and then smoothed the fabric down my arms. His smell was in the air instantly, along with his frustration. His hands gave me a gentle squeeze before he released me.

I turned around and looked at him again, finding him even more beautiful in the shadows than I did in the restaurant. The light from the streetlamp hit his face perfectly, bringing a special color to his eyes. His arms hung by his sides, and he kept a few inches of space between us. "You're right. You're not my kind of woman."

I refused to take that as an insult.

"That's why I like you."

I tightened my coat across my body, trapping the warm air against my body.

"You don't know anything about me. But you're right, I'm not a good guy. I'm not the man you'll marry. I won't give you four kids. But I will give you the most fun you'll ever have, the kind of sex that'll make your toes curl. Until you meet the guy you're looking for, I can be every-thing else you need in the meantime. Don't waste more time with guys like Samuel. Go to bed with a real man. Go to bed with me." His arms remained by his sides, but they shook slightly with restraint. His gaze was intense, borderline desperate. He was used to getting his way, but with me, getting what he wanted wasn't simple.

I shouldn't even want to agree to this, but I was standing there in the freezing cold wishing he would make me warm. Bosco was the last guy I should be with, but the idea of finding someone else was unappealing. All I would do was think about him, as my date with Samuel proved.

There was a mutual understanding that this would be meaningless. Sex was the only thing I wanted him for, and it seemed to be the only thing he wanted me for.

When nothing was said, he spoke again. "Let me take you home."

I stepped closer to him, unable to resist the magnetic pull between us. I wanted to inhale his scent, smell it as it was mixed with sweat. I wanted to taste his skin as well as his lips, claw at his back until I sliced the skin. My hands moved to his stomach, feeling his abs through the fabric of his suit. "As long as you're gone before morning."

4

BOSCO

WE SAT side by side in the back of the car as my driver drove to her apartment. I never asked for her address because I already knew exactly where she lived.

She didn't seem surprised.

I looked out the window into the darkness, but I was actually looking at her reflection in the glass. A few strands of hair framed her face, and she was exceptionally beautiful. With those beautiful cheeks, full lips, and those bright green eyes, she was one hell of a fantasy. That dark hair contrasted against her slightly olive skin. She was almost a foot shorter than me, but with long legs like that, she seemed much taller. She had the hourglass figure of a model, perfect waistline, perfect ass, and perfect tits.

I couldn't wait to fuck her.

I'd been thinking about it since the first time I'd kissed her.

The thought consumed me constantly. She was the one woman I couldn't have, the one woman who didn't give a damn about me. The only way I could convince her to sleep with me was if I proved to her how detached it could be.

She made it clear she didn't want me for any other reason.

Not once did she ask how I made my money. Not once did she ask how many people I'd killed. Not once did she ask me something even remotely personal.

Because she didn't give a damn.

She was a smart woman who didn't want to waste her time on a man who would never be good enough for her.

I respected that—immensely.

All the women in my life seemed to want more. One night was never enough. And when there were multiple nights, they only got more attached. But those were the kind of women that were impressed by my ironclad authority. They wanted to be my queen, stand by my side as I ruled this city.

Carmen didn't give a damn.

The driver stopped in front of her apartment, and we made our way up to the third floor and into the thousand-square-foot apartment where she lived alone. It was decorated in the same style as her flower shop, with pink couches and a blue coffee table. It was a design that could be ripped out of home decorating catalog. She flicked on the lights then let her heavy coat fall down her arms before she hung it up on the coatrack.

Her black dress was backless, showing the small muscles that flanked her spine. The steep curve in her back was prominent, so sexy I accidentally bit the inside of my cheek as I stared at it. I unbuttoned the jacket of my suit as I came up behind her, my mouth hungry for that beautiful skin.

I gripped both of her arms as my lips moved to the back of her neck. The second my mouth was on her body, I was lost. My hands squeezed her limbs, and I kissed her hard, devouring her in the entryway. I pulled her against my chest as my kisses migrated more toward her face. I tugged her against me and forced her head back, exposing more of her neck to my reach. My warm breaths fell on her skin as I kissed her, letting my cock grind against her ass through my slacks. I'd been hard on and off all night, and now my dick was about to rip through my pants.

She panted right away, arching her back and pushing into me as she let me have her. She wanted me to take her, practically begged me to. In just that short amount of time, I could tell she was an experienced woman, the kind that wasn't afraid to tell a man exactly how she liked to be pleased.

I kissed the shell of her ear before I whispered against it, "Fucking beautiful." I yanked on her arm and turned her around, my hand sliding into her hair as my other arm hooked around her waist. I pulled her against my chest then kissed her hard on the mouth.

She kissed me even harder.

I guided her backward down the hall toward the bedroom, my hands feeling this woman more intimately than I had before. Now that I knew how this would end, I gripped her a little tighter, kissed her a little harder. Every embrace was pleasurable, erotic foreplay that would lead to the kind of sex we would never forget. I backed her up farther until we entered her bedroom.

She cupped my face and kissed me the way she did in the alleyway, her lips giving me purposeful kisses that blew my mind. Never sloppy and never slow, she had perfect timing. Her soft lips were so full, perfect to suck into my mouth and wrap around my cock. She pushed my jacket off my shoulders and let it fall to the floor before she yanked on my tie. Like she'd done this many times, she had no problem getting my tie off. In fact, she removed it quicker than I could.

Her fingers went to my shirt next, quickly unfastening each button while our kisses never slowed. She pushed the shirt over my shoulders next and let it hit the floor at the foot of her bed. Her mouth was suddenly yanked from mine, and she looked down at my chest.

The heat had been severed because she'd ended it without warning. It seemed like she'd changed her mind, like she'd realized this was a mistake she couldn't live with. But then the desire burned in her eyes, and she dragged her hands down my chest, feeling the hardness of my pecs and then my abs. Slowly, she moved, biting her bottom lip in the process.

Jesus Christ.

I always made a woman feel sexy. But a woman had never made me feel so sexy.

Her fingers trailed the riverbeds in my abs, touching the hard muscle that a thousand daily crunches produced. Lower, her fingertips went until she reached the top of my slacks. Her hands were steady as she unfastened the button and got the zipper down. She took her time, purposely torturing the both of his. Then her tongue swiped across her bottom lip, like the sight of my body had been everything she'd ever wanted.

She gripped my slacks and my boxers and slowly tugged them down as she lowered herself to her knees in front of me, her dress rising over her hips and settling above her waist. Her toned thighs were exposed, along with the teal color of her panties.

She pulled my bottoms down until they were around my ankles then stared at my cock with the same desire she gave the rest of me. "Oh...wow." Her hands glided up my muscular thighs until she gripped my hips. Slowly, she leaned in and pressed a kiss to the head of my cock, giving him a slow and seductive greeting.

Who the fuck was this woman?

She dragged her tongue over the head, tasting the drool I had developed for her. She shut her mouth and enjoyed the taste before she did it again, getting my head wet with her saliva.

Head wasn't even this good when I paid for it.

She opened her mouth and flattened her tongue before she pushed her mouth past the head of my cock.

She closed her eyes for a moment, like she was enjoying the way my thickness stretched her throat.

I thought she'd be on the bed by now and we'd be fucking.

But this was good too.

She pushed my length as deep as she could go without losing her breath before she pulled it out again. Slowly, she moved, pressing her tongue hard against me and carefully keeping her mouth wide apart to keep the edge of her teeth away from my length. She sucked my cock like she enjoyed it, enjoyed everything from the size to the taste.

When I slid my hand into her soft hair, her eyes flicked up and looked at me.

Holy fuck.

Bright green orbs stared into mine, her arousal on fire. She didn't skip a beat as she continued to push my length into her throat, slowly so she could treasure every single inch. Her hands moved to my balls, and she gently massaged them with her soft fingertips.

My hand tightened on her hair, and I forgot to breathe. I'd been sucked off a lot in my life, but never quite like this. Her pressure was perfect, and even though she moved so slow, it felt so right. Her mouth was warm and soft, and she took extra care to make sure he felt welcome between those pretty lips.

She moved a little farther and pushed an extra inch inside, taking as much as she possibly could. She left a few inches of my base out, but that was still better than most women could handle.

With my feet shoulder-width apart, I gradually moved with her, giving her my dick at the same pace as she took it. She was getting me so wet, and I suspected I was doing the same to her. A woman didn't suck dick like that unless she loved every second of it.

She sucked on the head of my cock before she swiped her tongue across it. When she pulled off her mouth, there was a strand of saliva between her lips and the tip of my cock. She swiped it away with her tongue, never taking her eyes off me. This woman was so confident, so comfortable in her own skin, and that was the sexiest thing ever. Some women tried to pretend to be something they weren't, tried to be confident and cool to impress me, but they were never comfortable in their own shoes. This woman truly didn't give a damn what anyone thought of her.

She gripped my hips and pressed a soft kiss to the head of my cock, like she was giving him a tender good-bye. Sitting with her knees folded underneath her and her bright thong visible, she looked too perfect to be real.

She grabbed my hands and pulled herself up before she turned around and slid her hair over one shoulder, showing me the zipper to the back of her dress.

But all I was looking at was her perky ass in that blue thong. Two perfect cheeks that reminded me of plump nectarines, the color of her skin was gorgeous in comparison to that small piece of fabric. I breathed against her hair as I stared at it, feeling like a teenage boy who was getting pussy for the very first time.

I finally grabbed the top of the zipper and pulled it down, moving over the steep curve of her ass and to the bunched fabric where her dress was shoved up. I yanked it down to finish, and the dress opened and fell down her front.

Her naked back was beautiful, a perfect spine flanked by small muscles that shifted under the skin every time she moved. Flawless and untouched, it was the perfect receptacle for my kisses. I started at the back of her neck then kissed her shoulders, my fingers playing with the lace of her thong. I wrapped the material around my digit, adjusting it slightly so I could see the top of her ass. Instead of kissing her more, I could have pushed her onto the bed and sunk between her legs, but I loved taking my time. I loved exploring every inch of this exquisite woman.

I grabbed her hips and turned her around, seeing her in nothing but her thong and heels. The second I saw her perky tits, I inhaled a deep breath like I'd never seen boobs in my life. With perfect shape, perfect roundness, and perfect nipples, they were the hottest pair of tits I'd ever seen. They were big enough to fill the palm of my hands. "Jesus fucking Christ." I lifted her up so her tits were right in my face. I gripped her ass cheeks as I held her against my waist and kissed the valley between her breasts.

She hooked her legs around my waist and dug her hand into my hair, breathing hard as I harshly sucked her nipples into my mouth.

They tasted like honey and smelled like flowers. My tongue devoured every inch of her beautiful rack, my face getting lost in the soft cushion of her perkiness. I loved every feature on a woman, but her perfect tits suddenly made me a boob man.

I carried her to the bed, my knees sinking into her mattress as I gently laid her back onto the pillows. My lips pulled her tit into my mouth again as my hand pushed off her right heel. I did the same with the other shoe before I got a handful of her thong.

I leaned back and rested on the balls of my feet as I pulled the last piece of material off her body, over her shapely thighs and sexy knees. She bent her legs so I could get them down to her ankles and off her body.

In the center of her thong, I could see how wet she was. I stared at the shiny material before my eyes met hers.

There wasn't a hint of shame. She looked back at me fiercely, like she wanted my cock to feel just as how wet she was.

I wrapped the thong around my length and smeared her arousal all over me.

She took a deep breath, her nipples hardening like the end of a pencil.

I kept my gaze locked on hers as I rubbed myself, feeling her warm stickiness coat me from head to base.

She was so fucking wet that there was enough to make my entire dick shine.

I left the panties on the bed then widened her legs so I could get a taste directly from the source. My mouth kissed her entrance without giving her much warning, and as soon as my lips were on her, she rolled her head back and moaned.

"Bosco."

My tongue swiped her clit the second I heard my name on her tongue. I'd heard my name shouted by beautiful women before, always in the heat of passion, but it never sounded quite as good as when she said it. Her moan was accompanied by a wince of pain, as if she was so aroused it was actually painful. If she didn't come soon, she would explode.

I took my time kissing her pussy, getting acquainted with the territory I would mark as my own. My tongue moved inside her entrance, and I tasted her arousal. Flooded with lubrication, she didn't need my saliva to get her slick. I wanted to taste her anyway, to enjoy her the way she'd just enjoyed me.

She arched her back and writhed on the bed, her arousing performance on display. Her fingers dug into my hair, and she ground her bottom against my mouth, aggressively taking exactly what she wanted.

Sexy.

I knew she wanted to come against my face, and she was almost there. But I had other plans for her.

When she was about to come, I pulled my mouth away and licked her taste from my lips.

She released a growl of frustration. "Bosco..."

I moved off her and prepared to fetch my slacks from the floor.

"Wait." She grabbed my arm and pulled me back on top of her. Then she opened her nightstand and fished out a condom. I got a peek inside the drawer and saw a pile of at least twenty of them, along with her birth control pills and a few pieces of jewelry. She ripped the packet then pushed the condom over my head and gently rolled it to the base, just like an instructor in a health class. But she kept her eyes on me, her fingers doing all the work.

I didn't know what was sexier, the way she knew how to use a condom or the fact that she had her nightstand stuffed with foil packets. She took control of her sexual encounters, inviting lucky men to her apartment for a passionate night of sex with a goddess.

And I got to be one of those lucky men.

I got to fuck this queen.

I positioned myself farther on top of her, my chest pressing against her wet tits and my muscular thighs separating her slender legs. My narrow hips fit perfectly between her inner thighs, and my hand guided the tip of my cock to her entrance. I felt the moisture right at her entrance and sank into her, slowly pushing through her tightness and delving deeper into this soaked pussy.

Fuck.

She clawed at me right away, her eyes burning with immense desire. She gripped the back of my neck and yanked on my hair, moaning quietly in my face as she felt the inches gradually stretch her wide apart.

I kept going, slowly making my way into this perfect pussy. I could feel how wet and tight she was, feel the way her body responded to mine. She gripped my length like she never wanted it to leave.

When I was balls deep, I stopped on top of her, enjoying the feeling of our bodies combined together. I'd wanted to fuck her since I had her pinned against that wall in the alleyway, my hard dick rubbing against her clit. I'd been thinking about it ever since, smelling the stain on my jeans before jerking off.

I held my face above hers, seeing the same satisfaction in her gaze that was in mine. I hadn't even started fucking her yet, and it was still the best sex I'd ever had. She wanted me so much. I could feel it in the way she squeezed me, like she was already about to come.

Not caring about the taste of her pussy on my lips, she kissed me, her hand deep in my hair. She sucked my bottom lip and then gave me her tongue, swirling it with mine as her pussy tightened around me. She ended the kiss but didn't pull her mouth away. "Fuck me." The words emerged as a sexy whisper, an order from a beautiful commander. She looked me in the eye as she said it, having all the authority of a queen.

It was the one time I wanted to obey.

I rocked into her slowly, taking my time as I treasured

the feeling of our bodies sliding past one another. She was soaking wet, so there was plenty of lubrication between us. I glided through her, the walls of her pussy clenching me with the strength of an iron fist. I ground against her every time I was balls deep, hitting her clit with my pelvic bone to give her an extra burst of pleasure.

She started moaning like crazy, like she couldn't keep her mouth shut for longer than a second. She hooked her arms around my body and clung to my shoulders, her green eyes on me and her mouth open as she breathed. She kept her legs spread wide apart, giving me ample room to fuck her deeply. "Yes..." She bit her bottom lip as her tits shook with my thrusts. "Like that." She gripped my ass cheek and pulled me harder into her, telling me exactly what spot she wanted me to hit.

Fuck, she was beautiful. Telling me exactly what she wanted without a hint of hesitation was so damn sexy. Unafraid of her sexuality, she wasn't shy about telling a man exactly how she wanted to be fucked.

"Yes..." She closed her eyes for a second, biting her bottom lip so hard she might bleed. She dug one hand into her hair as she writhed through the pleasure, preparing for the bomb about to explode between her legs.

It was the sexiest performance I'd ever seen.

"Yes...right there." She opened her eyes again and looked at me, hitting her trigger hard, like a train crashing into a brick wall. Just as in the alleyway, her eyes danced with the same fire. But this time, it was an inferno, and she screamed so loud that all of her neighbors knew she was getting fucked right next door. "Bosco..." She held my gaze through the climax, her fingers pressing into my chest and slipping against my sweat. She widened her legs a little farther so I could fuck her harder, make the orgasm last as long as possible. "Yes...yes." She bit her bottom lip again and rode the climax until it was completely finished. Her fingers relaxed against my chest, and her teeth stopped digging into her lip. The blaze in her eyes slowly died down, and her pussy stopped bruising me with its tight squeeze.

"Beautiful." I widened her legs and deepened the angle, fucking her harder now that her climax had passed.

She cupped my cheek and kissed me, giving me a hot embrace full of tongue. "Make me come again." She spoke between our kisses, her tone deep and sexy. She wasn't afraid to ask for what she wanted. Made me wonder if she'd been with men who could even pull that off, or she just knew I was man enough to make it happen. I chose to believe it was the latter.

I sucked her bottom lip before I shifted my gaze back to hers. "I'll always make you come twice."

I LAY BESIDE HER AND CAUGHT MY BREATH, MY ENTIRE BODY coated with a thick film of sweat. I'd filled the condom with so much come, it seemed like it might rip. It was such a good orgasm, so sharp and violent. My entire body convulsed, and it brought me such pleasure that I was immediately exhausted afterward.

She was one hell of a woman.

Now I stared at her ceiling as she lay beside me, turned over on her side facing the opposite way. She didn't try to cuddle with me. She didn't say a single word at all.

I ran my fingers through my hair and tried to understand what had just happened.

I'd had the hottest sex of my life. It didn't involve whips or chains, and it didn't require a special position. It was missionary and right to the point, straight fucking with a condom. But this woman made something mediocre incredible.

I was definitely gonna fuck her again.

When I'd cooled off a bit, I got out of bed and pulled my clothes back on. I let the tie sit around my neck and didn't bother tying it back up. My driver knew exactly what I was doing in this apartment, so there was no reason to hide it.

Carmen didn't ask me to stay. She didn't look at me as she lay there, like she was trying not to fall asleep. Naked and beautiful, she was the most erotic image I'd ever seen, a woman sexually fulfilled.

I pulled my jacket over my arms and buttoned the front.

When I was completely ready, she got out of bed and

pulled on a new thong from her drawer. Then she walked past me and headed to the doorway.

I watched her go, staring at her perfect body as her hips swayed back and forth. With an hourglass figure and gorgeous legs, she was a sexy angel without wings. Once I recovered from the heavenly vision I'd just seen, I followed her.

She stood behind the open door, ready to get rid of me right away. Her eyes had a sleepy look to them, like she wished she could go straight to bed without even letting me out. She wanted to push me out of her apartment as quickly as possible. She got what she wanted, and now she had no other use for me.

Fucking hot.

"Good night." She grabbed the front of my shirt and yanked me toward her behind the privacy of the door and gave me a quick kiss on the mouth. Her soft lips gently caressed mine, less aggressive than they were earlier. She gave me a small amount of tongue before she released me.

I scanned her sexy body up and down, unable to look away from her beautiful curves and womanly perfection. How could I walk out and turn my back when I knew this was on the other side of that flimsy door? "Good night." The second I stepped over the threshold, she shut the door and locked it behind me. Her footsteps sounded as she returned down the hall, probably headed right to bed.

She didn't ask when she would see me again. Didn't

ask for my phone number. She got what she wanted, and once she was done, she stopped thinking about me entirely. She was the kind of woman that didn't need a man.

And that made her the perfect woman.

5

CARMEN

"Someone got laid last night." Vanessa appeared at the counter in my flower shop, wearing a loose sweater that hid her baby bump from view. Her hair was pulled back, and a red scarf was tied around her neck. The most obvious thing about her was the enormous rock that sat on her left hand.

"What makes you say that?" I dropped the pen on the counter and pushed the order sheet to the side.

"Because of that smile. It's the same smile I wear every day."

She was right on the money. "You got me."

"And the sex was good, I take it?"

Now I really couldn't stop smiling. "Unbelievable."

"Ooh...who is this guy?" She leaned farther over the counter, her eyes wide with interest. "Can we talk about it over lunch? The baby has been hungry nonstop all day."

I rolled my eyes. "Is the baby actually hungry? Or is that an excuse so you can eat whatever you want?"

She shrugged. "Both."

We went to a restaurant around the corner and sat by the window. I ordered a salad and an iced tea, and Vanessa ordered a sandwich and an extra plate of fries.

"The baby is craving fries, so I've been eating them constantly."

"Again, the baby or you?"

She rolled her eyes and sipped her water. "Let's stop talking about my cravings and talk about yours. So, who is this guy?"

"His name doesn't matter." He would never be anything more than sex, so I wasn't even going to mention his name to anyone. "But I call him Panty Soaker."

She clapped her hands together and laughed at the same time. "Wow, this guy sounds like a dream."

"In bed, yes. But he's also a huge asshole."

"Not the worst thing in the world. Griffin was an asshole when we first met."

I had a feeling our story wouldn't end up like theirs. "He's just not my type. He's not looking for his type either, so it's fine. There's this chemistry between us...it's like an inferno. I didn't want anything to do with him and told him to disappear, but he offered sex...so I took it. I have no regrets."

"Is he the best you've ever had?"

"Yes." My answer came out quicker than my next heartbeat. "But I'll never tell him that."

"Smart move." She drank her ice water, the only thing she could drink now that she was in the second trimester of her pregnancy. "Don't let his ego get any bigger."

"I don't think it can get any bigger."

She laughed again. "You sound like you really hate him. What did this guy do?"

"You know, the usual. A pissing contest. I was on a date with a guy, and he crashed it—chased my date away."

"Geez, that is a dick move. Were you having a good time?"

"No, not really. That's how he justifies it. Says I looked bored."

"Were you bored?" Vanessa countered.

"A bit."

"Were you gonna see that guy again?"

"No, probably not."

Vanessa shrugged. "Then maybe he did save you some time."

I rolled my eyes. "He acted like a dick. We both know it."

"I won't refute that," she said. "But it's not like you were having dinner with your soul mate or something. What else did he do?"

I didn't want to tell Vanessa the truth, not because I was afraid she would tell Bones even if I asked her not to.

I just didn't want anyone to know I was sleeping with a criminal. I didn't want to admit I couldn't find a nice guy who was also good in a bed, a man I was deeply attracted to. Vanessa wouldn't judge me since she'd been in a worse situation with Griffin, but I didn't want to be honest with myself—since I would judge myself. "He's just not right for me. I'll leave it at that."

I WAS WORKING IN THE SHOP WHEN GRIFFIN CALLED ME.

"Hey, what's up?" I tucked the phone between my shoulder and ear while I clipped the thorns off the stems. "I went out with Vanessa yesterday, and she ate an entire basket of fries. Don't tell her I told you."

He chuckled slightly. "Good. She needs to eat more."

"Oh, she's definitely eating more." Anytime I was around her, all she wanted to do was eat. Her pregnancy had increased her appetite like crazy. "That baby is gonna come out all cute and fat. What do you want? A boy or girl?"

"It doesn't matter to me."

"No preference?" I asked in surprise. "You seem like the kind of guy who wants a boy."

"If we have a daughter, she'll look like Vanessa...and I like that idea."

"Aww," I said under my breath. "That's sweet. So, what are you calling for? Just to chitchat?"

"You know I'm not a big talker."

"Yeah, I picked up on that," I said with a chuckle.

"Just wanted to make sure Bosco wasn't bothering you."

The playful banter between us died away instantly. I stopped clipping the flowers and set the shears on the counter, losing my concentration at the mention of his name. Just a few days ago, he was buried between my legs and we were both shaking because the sex was so magnificent. Maybe he had good sex like that all the time, but I certainly didn't. I still didn't know anything about Bosco, but I knew he was a serious opponent. I didn't want to stir up shit between him and Griffin. "Nope. Haven't seen him." I felt bad lying to Griffin like that, but I didn't want to get him involved. Even if I told him our relationship was consensual, he would probably still flip out. I'd seen him angry before, and I never wanted to see that look again.

"Good. Glad to hear it. Still being safe?"

"Of course." At least that was true.

"Alright. Just wanted to check. Let me know if you need anything."

It was sweet that he looked after me the way he did with Vanessa. Since he wasn't actually my brother, the gesture was even more touching. He wasn't responsible for my well-being, but that didn't change anything. He was protective without being overbearing, something my father had never been able to accomplish. "I will."

"Bye." He hung up without waiting for my response.

I set the phone down and got back to work.

"Hey, beautiful." His masculine voice nearly made me jump ten feet in the air. I didn't even realize he was in the store with me because I'd been too absorbed in the conversation with Griffin to notice. I'd let my guard down when it mattered most.

I looked up to see him standing on the other side of the counter, dressed in a gray V-neck with a black blazer. He wore denim jeans that fit snugly around his hips. Stubble was thicker on his face than it'd been the other night when we were together, but his eyes were just as vibrant as before. Colorful and hypnotizing, they could charm a snake with that look. He could certainly charm me. "Stop sneaking up on me."

"Start paying attention to who comes into your store." Like before, he gripped the edge of the counter and stared me down, perfectly comfortable with intense direct eye contact. If I refused to speak, he would keep staring at me for hours on end. My hostility had no effect on him.

"Is there something I can help you with?"

He nodded to the arrangement I was working on. "Who's that for?"

"The display window." I placed the flowers inside, the purple roses mixing with the large white flowers. It was a springtime arrangement, even though we were in the heart of winter.

"It's for sale, then?"

"Yes."

"I'll take it." He opened his wallet and threw the cash on the counter.

"That was a quick sale." I pushed the vase toward him and took the money. "Who's it for this time?"

The corner of his mouth lifted in a smile. "Jealous?"

"I don't get jealous. Just making conversation."

"I think if you saw me with another woman, you would be jealous."

"Really?" His arrogance never stopped surprising me. "Prove it, then."

He continued to smile, like this was some weird joke. "Trust me, you don't want me to do that."

I rolled my eyes. "Have a good day." I tried to dismiss him even though I knew it wouldn't work.

"You lied to him." He moved his hands into his pockets as he watched me. "Good choice."

"I didn't want to worry him."

"And he definitely would have worried. He would have marched down to my building and got himself shot. Or better yet, thrown in the ring."

I refused to asked what the *ring* meant. "My personal life is none of his business. He asked if you were bothering me—and I told him the truth."

That charming smile wasn't going to disappear anytime soon. "I knew you liked me."

I just liked what we could do between the sheets. "Is there anything else I can help you with?"

"All business, huh?"

"Well, it's rude to bother me at my place of business."

"Oh, so I am bothering you?" He stepped closer to the counter and invaded my space, made his presence feel so large that the solid table between us wasn't thick enough to keep us apart. He tilted his head slightly to the side, watching all the minor reactions on my face.

I hated myself for loving his confidence, the way he could enter any room and own it. I hated the way I despised everything about him but my legs still wanted to fall apart. I hated those beautiful blue eyes and the way they stared into mine when they watched me come. I hated that I wanted someone who was so wrong for me. "I don't come into your office, so you shouldn't come into mine."

"You're welcome to stop by anytime you want. I'd love to fuck you on my desk."

And just like that, the air left my lungs as the excitement took over. I'd been out with handsome men who were charming, but I'd never felt this kind of passion with anyone. Men never made me tremble the way this guy did. "I'll pass."

He made his way around the table until he was on my side of the counter. Then he stepped into me, invading my space by pressing his chest against my shoulder. He stared down at me, the breaths from his nose hitting the top of my head. "Why don't I believe you?"

Because he wasn't stupid. "I need to get back to work." I moved away from his chest, keeping my guard up around this dangerous man. "There's only one thing I want from you, so I don't want to see you at my shop again." A part of me felt cold for blowing him off so harshly, but if I knew if I were a man, no one would think twice about it.

"Right to the point, huh?" he asked with a chuckle, unaffected by my rejection.

I grabbed a business card and flipped it over. I scribbled my phone number with a black marker and then pushed it back toward him. "Text me."

He didn't grab the card, his eyes still focused on me with laser-sharp intensity. "Is this a booty call situation now?"

"It was always a booty call situation." Griffin stopped by occasionally, as did my father and uncle. It would be impossible for me to explain Bosco's presence without telling the truth. After everything Vanessa went through with Griffin, I wasn't eager to repeat that. "Goodbye, Bosco."

He took the card and put it in his front pocket. "Bye, Beautiful." He moved to my side again, this time turning his face so he could give me a kiss. But he didn't lean all the way in, just hovered inches away. His cologne wrapped around me like an envelope around a letter, and his icy blue eyes bore into mine with daring aggression. He didn't make the last move, coaxing me into doing it.

When I didn't kiss him back, he pulled away. "Thank you for the flowers." He moved past me and grabbed the vase and set them in front of me. "They're for you." He turned away quickly, not caring about my reaction to the gesture.

I stared at his muscular back, remembering the way I'd dug my nails into his ripped muscles. I'd yanked him harder into me when I wasn't getting enough, and he delivered. I'd already known the sex would be perfect based on our hot embrace in the alleyway, but he'd still exceeded my expectations.

I should keep up my guard and let him walk away, but I felt my body soften with regret as I watched him go. "Bosco."

He stopped in front of the door but didn't turn around. "Yes?"

My heels clacked against the floor as I approached him from behind. I stopped when my face was nearly pressed against his shoulder blades.

He turned around then, trying to fight the smile that was coming over his mouth. "I knew you weren't gonna let me walk out of here." While keeping his eyes on me, he locked the front door then dug his hand into my hair. He pressed his soft lips against mine and kissed me in front of the window, fisting my hair like it was reins and I was his horse. His other arm wrapped around my waist, and he pulled me into him, keeping me warm with his hot and hard body.

The second our mouths touched, I was lost to the passion and chemistry our bodies created. My hands moved to his shoulders, my favorite feature of his physique, and I sucked his bottom lip into my mouth. I didn't want to feel him slip from my fingertips, not when this felt so good.

He ended the embrace first, having the strength I lacked. That soft smile was on his lips, like he'd just won some kind of game. "I knew you didn't hate me." He kissed the corner of my mouth. "Not when you kiss me like that."

I THREW AN EXTRA LOG ON THE FIRE BECAUSE THE FLAMES were starting to die down. It was freezing that night, so cold that my furnace couldn't keep up with the constant cold. The wind had a stinging bite to it, and the second I was home, I knew I wasn't going out again, not until the morning when I had to go to work.

I sat in the armchair in my living room and let the heat from the fire thaw out my toes. I wore thick wool socks, but that wasn't enough for these freezing temperatures. It was one of the coldest winters Florence had ever had, and some people thought it would snow this season, even though it hardly ever snowed here.

My phone lit up with a text message from a number I didn't recognize. But the message itself told me exactly who it was. *Can I come in?*

The hair on the back of my neck immediately stood on end. Just when I thought I was alone with the silence that wrapped around me, I realized I was wrong. Not only was he on my doorstep, but he somehow knew I was home. *I'm surprised you even asked.*

I don't have to ask. The sound of the opening door reached my ears a second later. The knob was locked, along with the security bar at the top. But he managed to get through it without any issue.

I was in my sweatpants, a baggy sweater, and thick old-lady socks, but I didn't have any time to prepare for the beautiful man entering my apartment. I shut the book I was reading and set it on the table beside me, next to the hot mug of tea I'd been sipping

His footsteps sounded in the kitchen, his heavy weight audible in every single step. He turned the corner, his eyes moving to me like he knew exactly where I was before he stepped inside the apartment.

I rose to my feet and held myself with the same dignity I always possessed. I didn't care that I was dressed in baggy clothes with no makeup. He only gave me five seconds of warning before he barged into my apartment like he had every right to do whatever he wanted. I tucked my hair behind my ear then crossed my arms over my chest, meeting his beautiful gaze with the same confidence he showed. "I hope you didn't break my locks."

"No." His eyes roamed over my body like I was in lingerie rather than baggy clothes. He seemed to want me the same way, whether I wore makeup or not. The tension rose between us, and it felt like he couldn't wait to get his hands on me. "But if you really want to be safe, you need an upgrade."

"Any recommendations?"

"Yes." He moved closer to me and slipped his hand under the fall of my hair. "Me." He bent his neck down and kissed me, his anxious lips taking mine like they were his property. He sucked my bottom lip aggressively before he gave me purposeful kisses, embracing me tenderly, then deeply a moment later. His kisses were never predictable, packed with passion that sucked me deep into him. His hand snaked around my hair, and he got a good grip of it, like there was any possibility I would try to run away.

No, I was stuck.

With his back to the fire, he continued to kiss me, his long-sleeved shirt covering the tanned skin of his arms and chest. The cool metal of his watch grazed my skin as he kissed me, but the longer we touched, the warmer it started to feel.

His arm circled around the deep curve in my back, and he pulled me hard against him, making sure I could feel the outline of his rigid cock through his jeans. My baggy sweater and loose pants didn't quench his fire at all. He moved his hand underneath my sweater and touched the bare skin of my back, clutching me anxiously.

A man had never touched me this way, gripped me so hard that his arms started to shake. His kisses proved that he'd been thinking about me all day, waiting for the kiss we were sharing at that very moment. He probably kissed every woman like this, made every woman scream in pleasure while he was buried between her legs, and every time he left, they were heartbroken. But it was easy to believe that I was the only one he devoured this way, that I was somehow special.

The fantasy wasn't real, but it was fun to believe in.

He broke our kiss for a heartbeat just to remove his shirt. He dropped it on the ground and then smothered me with his hands once more, his ripped body as strong as ever. His fingers gently touched my neck, my hair, and my petite shoulders. He felt me everywhere, kissing me with increasing vigor.

My hands started at his shoulders, feeling the prominent grooves that separated the muscles between his shoulders and arms. The dips were significant because the muscle was so profound. My hands slid down his arms, hitting the enormous bump of his biceps, and kept going as I felt the individual cords along his forearms. Chiseled and defined, he was a living sculpture the Greek gods created themselves.

My hands moved to his chest next, feeling the searing warmth that was far hotter than the fire that burned just feet away. I felt his hard pecs, large slabs of muscle that felt like chunks of concrete. My fingers slipped down and felt his chiseled eight-pack, the lines of muscle on the beautiful tanned skin.

He kept kissing me while I explored him, like he knew his body was a form of foreplay.

He was so damn hot.

I'd been with some good-looking men, but none of them compared to this man. Perfect in every way, from the stubble across his jawline to his chiseled physique, Bosco was everything a woman wanted in a man. The only hint of light in his dark exterior was his exceptionally blue eyes. They were the color of a summer sky on a clear day—beautiful blue.

He gave me his tongue just before he pulled my sweater over my head.

I wasn't wearing anything underneath, not even a bra.

He stopped to look at me, his eyes enjoying the sight of my tits without shame. His hand was still deep in my hair, and a quiet moan escaped his lips. "Jesus." He dropped to his knees in front of me, his body hitting the rug that covered the hardwood floor. He gripped my hips and kissed my belly, his tongue swiping over the piercing I had in my navel. He kissed both of my hips and then made his way up my sternum, taking his time as he tasted me. His hands yanked down my sweatpants and revealed my long legs and my black thong. My underwear was the only remotely sexy thing I wore in my ensemble.

He kissed my thighs next before he moved his mouth right between my legs. The fabric separated his lips from my clit, but the pressure was still good enough to make my hips buck slightly.

The first time we'd slept together, he didn't hesitate

before he pressed his face between my legs. He devoured me like he was in a buffet line, sucking my clit and diving his tongue deep inside me. A man didn't usually do that until we'd been seeing each other for a while, but Bosco went for it right away.

It was so good. Just as good as the sex.

My fingers dug into his hair as I felt him kiss me through my panties. I'd been ready for him since the first minute of our kiss. Now I couldn't stop picturing him on top of me, thrusting into me, with those powerful muscles flexing and shifting. His huge dick was so good, stretched me in a way a man never had before. I panted just thinking about it, fantasizing about the man who was enjoying me that very moment.

He rose to his feet again, but this time, he lifted me into the air, putting my tits perfectly in line with his mouth. He sucked my left nipple into his mouth then gave me a nibble with his teeth. He did the same to the other, lavishing my tits with heated kisses. He was in love with my rack the way I was in love with his shoulders. Most men were particularly drawn to my tits because of their size and perkiness, and Bosco had the same reaction. He licked the valley between my tits then kissed them again, his cock throbbing against my clit.

He held me with one arm as he unbuttoned his jeans and pushed them down along with his boxers. He carried me to the couch and lay back, cradling me against him and keeping my pussy right against his dick. With my tits in his face, he kissed them again as he ground against me. "Fuck, I love your tits." He gave a gentle bite above my left nipple, breathing hard with arousal.

My pussy ground against his cock, and I felt his enormous thickness underneath me. He was the biggest man I'd ever had, possessing a girth that impressed me. People say size doesn't matter, but after sleeping with him, I knew that was bogus. He made me feel full the entire time, and he made me so wet that our bodies moved together easily. "I love your cock."

He lifted his gaze to meet mine, that dark expression becoming sexier by the minute. His jaw was clenched tightly, and his fingers dug into my hips so deeply he almost hurt me.

I lifted my body up to pull down my thong, but it only got so far.

"Here." He gripped the cotton with both hands and ripped the strap right off, the veins on his hand thickening with the exertion. He pushed the material away until it rested on his knee, and he yanked me down again, pressing me right against his cock. "Fuck..." He slowly ground against me, feeling my soaked pussy. My arousal smeared all over his length, coating him from below his tip to his base.

Instead of pulling on a condom, he kept grinding against me, tugging on my hips so I moved forward and backward. He stared at my tits for a while before he looked me in the eye, the sexual desire raging like a forest fire.

I planted my hands against his chest and continued to grind against him, rolling my hips slowly and pressing hard against him. His thickness was so hard that it felt perfect against my clit, the right pressure to drive me wild. I didn't even need him inside me to feel the climax start.

Bosco moved under me, grinding against me with equal desperation. Instead of kissing, we kept our eyes locked on one another, enjoying each other on an intimate level I'd never shared with another lover.

He gripped both of my tits with his large hands. "Fuck, you're so damn wet."

"For you." I didn't get this wet for just anybody. I'd never been this wet in my life, actually.

His eyes darkened like I'd just hit an invisible trigger. His fingers dug into me a little harder, his hips pushing into me with more pressure. "No condom." He didn't phrase it as a question, but he waited for my permission.

I was on birth control, but that was to regulate my cramps as well as an extra precaution. My family would be so disappointed in me if I ever got knocked up without being in a serious relationship. "I never let a man fuck me without a condom. You aren't any different, Bosco."

Instead of pissing him off, that seemed to turn him on even more. "Jesus, you're so sexy." He leaned forward and kissed my tits again, grinding me more firmly against his length.

I tilted my head back and pressed my body harder

into him, feeling the sweat start to drip down my back. There was so much wetness between us that we slid back and forth without friction.

My clit dragged down his wet length, and my body tightened as the pleasure radiated out from my body. I was surprised by an unexpected crescendo, a climax that made me buck and grind into him harder while he sucked my tits until they were raw. "Bosco..." I didn't care if it inflated his ego like a balloon. He made me come so easily, and he always made me come so hard. He deserved to hear his name on my lips, listen to the way he pleased me.

He sucked my nipple hard, giving it an aggressive bite as I rode the high down to the bottom. "Fuck, you just got wetter." He licked the valley between my tits and then leaned back against the couch, his breathing deep and ragged. He reached into the front pocket of his jeans that were still around his knees and fished out a foil packet. He ripped it open and then pulled his cock toward his stomach, his large fingers wrapped around his thick length.

I watched him roll the condom onto his long length, pinching the tip so he had plenty of room to place his load. He kept his eyes on me as he did, strategically getting the rubber in place by feel. When he was ready to go, he grabbed my hips and directed me down his length, his cock pushing through my arousal. He kept guiding me until I contained every inch of his length, his balls right under my ass.

My nails dug into his chest when I felt him, and after the intense climax I'd just had, I was surprised I wanted another. His thickness immediately recharged my batteries, refreshed my body so I could come all over his dick once more. "Make me come again." I didn't apologize for my selfishness. The reason we were doing this was because we were both selfish. We just wanted to have good sex, to screw without meaning, not to have to give any explanations.

He thrust up into me, hitting me deep and hard with his massive dick. "Yes, Beautiful."

AFTER I CLEANED UP IN THE BATHROOM, I PULLED ON A new thong and then walked into the living room, expecting Bosco to be gone because our fun was over. He'd made me come again, made me scream in his face because the climax was good, and then I'd watched him explode, watched his beautiful jawline become even tighter as he clenched his teeth.

Just watching him come turned me on all over again.

When I returned to the living room, he was on the couch in his boxers, his muscular thighs spread apart as he stared at the low burning fire. His broad shoulders dipped into the couch, and he rested his fingers along his jaw, feeling the stubble under his fingertips.

I'd expected him to be gone by now. "Want some water?"

"I'll take scotch, if you have it."

"Actually, I do." Now that the fun was over, I wanted him to leave my apartment so I could go to sleep, but I didn't want to be rude. He knew I didn't want him sleeping over, so he wouldn't try. I went into the kitchen and poured two glasses before I joined him on the couch.

The corner of his mouth rose in a smile. "I like a woman who has scotch on hand."

"My father drinks a lot of it. I prefer wine, but sometimes scotch hits the spot." I took a big drink before I set the glass on the coffee table. When I looked at the fire, I noticed the flames were burning brighter because he'd tossed another log onto the pile.

He drank his entire glass in one gulp before he set it on the table. He leaned back and wrapped his arm around my shoulders, pulling me gently into his side. His eyes glanced down to my tits. "You should dress like this all the time."

"I thought you would be gone when I walked into the living room."

"As long as you're showing off those tits, I'm not going anywhere." His hand moved into my hair and pulled it off my shoulder, revealing more of the side of my face. For a harsh man, he could be surprisingly gentle.

I grabbed the blanket off the back of the couch and wrapped it around myself, keeping warm in the cold apartment.

He didn't try to yank it off. "You have a nice place."

I was sure he lived in a mansion, but it was nice of him to say anyway. "Thanks."

He kept running his fingers through my hair as he turned his gaze toward the fire. He watched the flames dance around, the gentle cracking and random pops filling the silence of my apartment. The curtains were closed on all the windows, but I knew they were frosted from the cold.

I'd offered him a drink and a bit of chitchat, so now I didn't feel rude kicking him out. "I have to be up early tomorrow..."

He stared at the fire like he didn't hear a word I said. "You haven't asked me a single question about myself." After a long pause, he turned back to me, the orange flames reflecting in his blue eyes. "Not even my last name."

"Is your last name relevant?" I countered. "When we're screwing, I think your first name is sufficient."

He gave that lopsided grin, but it didn't last long. "My point still stands."

"I haven't asked anything because I don't want to know anything. Pretty simple."

"Bones didn't tell you everything about me?"

"No. He just said you control all the money...something like that. He said you aren't a trafficker, and that's all I really care about. The rest of your story doesn't matter because of the context of our relationship."

He watched the fire again.

"We're just screwing, so I don't need to know anything about you."

"You aren't even a little bit curious?" he said quietly.

"No." I didn't care about his criminal activities. I didn't care about his hobbies. I didn't care about anything other than his beautiful exterior.

"Someone hurt you, sweetheart?"

"No." I untangled myself from his arm and rose to my feet, keeping the blanket draped around me. "I would never let a man hurt me. This is just a physical relationship. I don't care where you sleep at night or what you do during the day. Call me heartless. Call me cold. I don't care. You're a criminal man who does illegal things, someone I would never introduce to my family. I would never consider keeping you around as anything more than a lover. It's pretty easy not to care about someone you know you'll never care about." I stared him down, seeing his side profile as he looked at the fire.

He slowly turned my way, his eyes empty and his jaw tight. "I've never met a woman like you." He rose to his feet and towered over me. He looked down into my face, his head slightly tilted to the side. Back and forth, his eyes shifted. "I've never had a woman use me this way. I've never had a woman be so pragmatic...so smart. You're right, I'm not good enough for you. I'm not a good man. I kill men every day...rule this city without a crown. I admire your sensibility in keeping your distance. A lot of women tell me the same thing, that just fucking is enough...but it never is. You're the first woman who's ever said it and actually meant it."

If he understood my viewpoint and even agreed with it, why was he still there? "Then you should get going." I turned away and grabbed my sweatshirt from the ground and pulled it over my head. I felt bad for all the women who ever thought getting involved with Bosco would be a good idea. He had heartbreaker written all over him. Not only was he dangerous to everyone he came into contact with, but he was dangerous to all women who got too close. He was untamable, a dreamy man with perfect looks and perfect moves. Any woman could picture him being the dream hunk she wanted to sleep beside her every night. I didn't blame him for putting all of them under his spell, but I certainly wouldn't repeat their mistakes.

He stood up and pulled on his clothes before he came up behind me. His arms moved to my hips, and he rested his chin on top of my head. "I'm a dangerous man from a dangerous world. I've done things you can't even imagine. But I want you to know I would never hurt you." He wrapped his arms around my chest and secured me in his grip. "Physically or emotionally. That's not a promise I make to anyone, only those who earn my respect. Beautiful, you've earned my respect a million times over." He released his grip and turned away, leaving me standing in front of the fire.

I'd never been afraid that he would hurt me. He'd always given me the luxury of making my own decisions.

Every time I said no, he listened. But just because he was kind to me didn't mean other people were so lucky. I kept my gaze on the fire and waited for the door to shut behind him.

"It's Roth, by the way." He shut the door behind him, and the silence ensued.

Bosco Roth.

I was sleeping with Bosco Roth.

6

BOSCO

I SAT at my black desk and stared at my laptop. The accounts were pulled up, all the money that was wired from members that afternoon. If people wanted to gamble at my casino, they had to pay their monthly dues. They weren't just paying for the games, but secrecy, privacy, booze, and of course, women.

Not just anyone could play here.

A knock sounded on the door, and I glanced at the screen on the wall to see who it was through the camera.

Ronan.

I hit the button and unlocked the door.

He stepped inside, dressed in a fitted t-shirt and jeans. His heavy boots thudded against the black tile as he made his way toward me. With identical blue eyes and the same tanned skin, my younger brother looked more like my twin. "There are four men down in the basement."

"A double feature, huh?"

"Yep. The men are too scared to rip us off, so our men are bringing in their own enemies are part of their initiation fee."

When men were stupid enough to cross us, we tossed them into the ring to fight for their lives. If they won, they got to keep their life and turn into my bitch. If they didn't...that was self-explanatory. It was an illegal fighting ring and how I made the bulk of my money. Men loved betting on the sport, and it was always entertaining. My cruelty was obvious to everyone in the underworld, so it was rare for someone to actually cross the casino. We were running out of fighters that way, so members volunteered their enemies—and they made a lot of cash because of it.

"Good. It'll be a great time." I shut my laptop even though Ronan knew about the cash because he ran this world with me. It was too big for one person, but I was definitely the one on top.

Ronan sat in the seat across from my desk, his muscular arms stretching his t-shirt. "I've got a new fish on the line. But I only hear bad things about this guy."

I rolled my eyes. "The same thing is true for every other member here. We're murderers, thieves, and tyrants. Why do you think we get along so well?" I leaned back against my leather chair and gave him a slight wink.

"But this guy is unpredictable. He's shifty."

"What did you hear?"

"They call him The Butcher. I guess he killed his whole family."

I shrugged. "I've wanted to do the same to you a few times."

Ronan didn't respond to my joke. "But he was fifteen when he killed his entire family—with a knife."

That was pretty damn bloody. "What does he do now?"

"That's the thing—nothing specific. He robs people at random, kills some of them. Has a group of thugs that follow his orders. He makes serious dough that way, robbing rich houses and threatening to kill their kids if they call the cops."

"Sounds like an angel compared to some of the assholes in here."

"But sometimes he doesn't take anything... Sometimes he butchers an entire family at random and just leaves..."

That made my blood turn cold. Criminals usually had a motive, and that made them easy to understand. When they only wanted one thing, they were easy to manipulate, to predict. But when there was no motivation, it was a different story. I'd killed a lot of men in my life, but never without provocation. And I'd never killed a woman or a child. Butchering innocent people had never been my thing, but I definitely wouldn't go out of my way to save them either. "Interesting."

"See what I mean? He's a loose cannon."

"You want to deny him entry?"

He shrugged. "Maybe."

"We have lots of killers here."

"Yeah, but they're predictable. They kill for a reason. This guy doesn't—which makes him a psychopath."

Turning down a psychopath was sometimes worse than letting him in—and keeping a close eye on him. "He understands the rules here. Regardless of the company he keeps, he'll never be able to challenge us. And if he does step out of line, we'll send him to the ring. I'm sure a lot of people would love to see him beaten to death."

"Unless he wins," he countered.

If he really was that much trouble, there were ways to get around it. "I'll make sure he doesn't."

———

I LAY BESIDE A WOMAN, FINISHED BUT UNSATISFIED.

She was beautiful and knew how to please a man, but I found myself bored most of the time, my mind drifting elsewhere.

To someone else.

There wasn't unbridled passion or scorching heat. There weren't tremors that shook my arms. There wasn't that slow burn that turned into a raging inferno. It was tame—ordinary. She came, and I only did because I made it happen.

Now I felt my body fill with regret, wishing I'd gone

somewhere else that night instead of taking this woman up on her offer.

I wasn't even sure what her name was.

Michelle?

Melanie?

Whatever, it didn't fucking matter.

I sat up in bed and ran my hand through my hair, wondering if Carmen was alone in her apartment right now. Was she sleeping with other men? Did she have regulars that she invited over? Or was I her number one choice? I would ask, but she rarely gave up personal information since she was insistent on keeping her distance from me.

Which was a wise decision.

What's-Her-Face ran her hand down my back. "Bosco?"

I ignored her.

"Come to bed."

If I wanted to be in bed with her, she wouldn't have to ask. "I need to get up early, so you should get going." Just as Carmen blew me off, I dismissed this woman with the same indifference. I rose to my feet and pulled on my boxers, annoyed all over again that Carmen could forget about me the instant I left her apartment. She never asked me to stay. The second she was finished with me, she disposed of me like an old condom.

Why did that make me so angry?

Was it just my ego?

Or was it something else?

"I'm too tired to get up," What's-Her-Name whispered, staying under my sheets.

I turned back to her, disgusted with her clinginess. "Don't make me ask you again." I threw her dress at her and walked out.

———

CARMEN WENT OUT THAT NIGHT WITH A FEW FRIENDS. They hung out a club for most of the night, drinking and dancing. It wasn't long after that when a good-looking guy worked up the courage to buy her a drink.

I sat in the corner, my dozen men spaced out around the club. I had a booth to myself, and anytime a woman tried to approach me, one of my men shooed her away. Carmen didn't notice since she was distracted by many other things.

One of my men took a scan of the guy's face and instantly relayed the information to me. "Early thirties. Divorced. Has a young daughter. Works as an assistant professor at the university. He teaches mathematics."

Basically, he was the most boring guy on the planet. "Thanks, Rio. Get rid of him." I stood up and straightened my leather jacket before I made my way across the room and to Carmen at the bar. I knew my men would get rid of the guy before I arrived, so I didn't take my time, ignoring the disappointed looks women gave me when I didn't notice them.

I approached her from behind, seeing her in a purple

dress with black heels. It fit her hourglass figure perfectly, the beautiful curve of her hips, and showed off her gorgeous long legs.

That guy didn't deserve five minutes of her time.

No, he didn't deserve a second of her time.

She stood there alone, a scotch in her hand.

It was so sexy that she drank scotch.

I brushed her shoulder as I passed, then stood in front of her, watching the surprise on her face when she realized it was me. But quickly, she covered it up, putting on an impressive poker face. "I sincerely hope you aren't the reason Pietro just left."

I grabbed her glass and took a drink. "I don't like to lie, so I'll just say nothing instead."

Her green eyes narrowed in instant hostility. "Bosco, this isn't funny."

"I'm not trying to make you laugh. You know I only like to make you come."

She kept up her angry expression, but I knew her rage had simmered down slightly. "I want you to leave."

"No, you don't." I moved closer to her, my chest nearly touching hers. I wrapped her in my cologne and my presence, letting her feel my immense power. I had this entire club under my control, and she didn't even realize it. My hand went to her waistline, and I gave her a gentle squeeze, reminding her she belonged to me even if she forgot. "He's divorced with a kid. That's not what you're looking for."

Her eyes narrowed again. "You had no right to tell

me that."

"I have the right to do whatever I want. I'm sure he was going to keep that information to himself as long as possible."

"So what?" she countered, her eyes flashing with irritation. "There's nothing wrong with being divorced and having a child."

"There's not. But that's not what you're looking for. You told me you want to fall in love with the right guy and spend the rest of your life with him. You aren't going to do that picking up a guy in a bar."

"An alleyway is better?"

"I never said I was the right guy. But I'm better than him. You really want to go home with some guy and have mediocre sex?"

"I don't screw every guy I meet. I usually have a date or two first, not that it's any of your business."

"Well, that wasn't going to go anywhere."

"How would I know?" she asked. "You run off every guy I talk to."

"And you're welcome."

Rage flashed in her eyes, and she moved for her glass, ready to throw it in my face.

I got there quicker, moving the glass out of her reach without taking my eyes off her. "Listen to me."

"Listen to you?" she hissed. "You literally watch every move I make. It's fucking annoying."

"I don't, actually. But it seems that way, doesn't it?"

"I like having my freedom, Bosco. I'm not going to let

you take it away from me."

"Let me remind you that the only reason you have any freedom is because of me." I stepped closer to her and hooked my arm around her waist. Even though she was angry with me, she never pushed away my touch. I knew that her anger only ran so deep, that she wanted me even if she wouldn't say it. "I could have kept walking, and you would be worse than dead right now."

"Only because you owed Griffin a favor—"

"Doesn't fucking matter." I grabbed the back of her neck and kept her gaze focused on me.

She didn't push me away.

"I was there that night. I was the one who saved you. You owe me, and we both know it."

Both of her eyebrows rose. "All I owe you is a thank you. I will not be your bitch, Bosco. I will never submit to a man as long as I live. Any man who has to ask for it is inherently weak."

My cock nearly burst out of my jeans because of that comment. I loved the fire in her eyes, the way she mouthed off to an opponent twice her size. I loved the way she cared so much about her dignity. I loved the way she didn't melt in my hands like the others did. She was better than that, smarter than that. A woman who didn't put up with bullshit was a very special kind of woman. "I wasn't asking, Beautiful."

"Seemed like it."

Just to prove how much power I had over her, I leaned in and kissed her.

She didn't kiss me back right away, her form of resistance, but slowly, her lips started to move and she even gave me her tongue.

I pulled her closer to me and made out with her right at the bar, proving my point a million times over. She could be angry with me all she wanted, but nothing I did would change what we had. We were like a plug and an outlet—we went together perfectly and created electricity.

I ended the kiss and stared at her, seeing the anger disappear from her face. "Will you listen to me now?"

"I've never been a very good listener."

My hand moved under the fall of her hair, and I let her feel my length as I pressed it against her, reminding her that this was the only cock she wanted inside her that night. "I want you to give me a chance."

"A chance for what?" she asked, genuinely bewildered by the question.

"A chance like you give these losers."

Her eyes narrowed once more, still not following my logic.

"I want a chance to be something more. I don't know what exactly, but I want something. Anything."

"Bosco, you aren't the kind of man I'm looking for."

"What?" I asked. "Powerful? Rich? Good in bed? You want an average guy who can give you an average life? You would rather have someone like Pietro than someone like me?" I refused to believe any woman would pick the latter.

"Where is this coming from?" she asked. "Everything seemed fine the other day, and now you're asking for something completely different than what we talked about." She stared at me with confusion written on her face.

I never hesitated to tell the truth, so I didn't hesitate now. "I slept with someone the other night."

She didn't react at all.

"She was nothing compared to you." I held her gaze and kept my arm around her waist, hoping this revelation wouldn't push her away. But at the same time, I wanted to see pain in her eyes, to know she would be jealous at the thought of me with someone else.

There was no sign of anything I wanted to see.

"It made me realize you're the only woman I want right now. That's never happened to me before."

She finally broke eye contact and looked away, scanning the other people in the bar. My words seemed to make her uncomfortable because she never looked away when I stared her down. She always held her own. "I don't want to get involved with someone like you."

"Beautiful, you don't know me."

"I want to keep it that way," she whispered. "That's the only way this works. I want a good guy."

"Good guys are overrated."

"I know what I want." She lifted her gaze and looked at me again.

"I'm not asking for forever." I kissed the corner of her mouth. "I'm just asking for some of you...for a while."

7

CARMEN

I DON'T KNOW what I was thinking.

Why did I say yes?

He had a valid point about the guys I'd been seeing. None of them got my blood pumping the way he did. They were definitely average...and a bit boring. None of them made me press my thighs together with desire. None of them made me tense when they walked through the door.

Why did the only guy I actually liked have to be a criminal?

What was wrong with me?

I did my best keeping him at a distance, keeping my feelings locked up in a safe inside my heart, but now that he was pursuing me harder, it was becoming difficult to ignore him. It was becoming difficult to pretend he meant nothing to me.

Truth be told, I was tired of going out to find

someone special, only to be disappointed time and time again. The rest of my family had settled down with the perfect partners, even Vanessa. Conway married a model and now had a kid, my brother had Mia, who was also lovely. And Vanessa had a man who loved her more than anything else in the world.

I was the only one alone.

Being alone never bothered me because there was a distinct difference between being alone and being lonely.

I never felt lonely.

But I did want that special man to spend the rest of my life with.

I was starting to wonder if he was really out there.

I was at home when Bosco called me.

I took a deep breath before I answered. "Hi." Now that the relationship was different, I didn't know how to talk to him. He wasn't my boyfriend. But he wasn't just some guy I was screwing anymore. I wasn't sure what he was.

He got straight to the point. "Have dinner with me tonight."

I stood in my living room with my arm wrapped around my waist. I'd been to dinner with dozens of guys, but none of those dates made me nervous. This one made me nervous as hell...because I had no idea what I was doing. "Alright."

"I'm outside whenever you're ready."

"Maybe you should ask ahead so you don't have to sit in the hallway forever."

"I'm not sitting in the hallway. I'm in the car on the street. One of my men will escort you." Click.

The man seemed to be chauffeured by two dozen men everywhere he went. I wondered if he would close down the restaurant like he did last time. That seemed over the top and unnecessary.

My hair and makeup were already done, so I pulled on a black cocktail dress and heels before I left my apartment. Just as Bosco said, there was a man in a suit waiting in the hallway for me. He walked ahead of me and guided me downstairs. He spoke into the intercom in his ear. "She's coming, sir."

I did my best not to roll my eyes.

Bosco was standing on the sidewalk next to his blacked-out car. There were two other cars in front of him and behind him, making him look like a president who was protected by the Secret Service. He stood with his hands in the pockets of his jeans. He wore a white V-neck and a black blazer, dressed nicely, but not overly nice. His eyes settled on me, and he looked at me with the same intensity he always watched me with, like he wanted to press me against the car and screw me then and there.

I walked up to him, feeling my heart beat fast in my chest. I was nervous, nervous that I'd agreed to do this.

His hands immediately circled my waist, and he leaned down to kiss me softly on the mouth. He pulled me closer as he deepened the kiss, claiming me right on the sidewalk and in front of his men. He gripped the fabric of my dress and made it rise a little higher.

I wanted to pull away first, but I couldn't. Hypnotized by his possessive kiss, all I could do was take it.

He finally pulled away and opened the back door for me.

I got inside, and he sat beside me. Then the car pulled forward, and we headed to our destination.

"I hope you aren't planning on closing down the restaurant like last time."

"That's the only way I dine." He faced forward, his knees wide apart with one arm propped on the windowsill. "I'm not a fan of people or the public."

"Well, people aren't fans of an asshole who shuts down their favorite restaurant."

He smiled slightly. "It really bothers you, huh?"

"I think it's a little excessive." Okay, not a little. Extremely excessive.

"Fine. Then I won't shut it down."

"Good."

He stayed on his side of the car and didn't try to hold my hand or give me any other kind of intimate affection. He didn't try to talk to me either.

I was still nervous, nervous that I was going on a real date with a man I knew I should stay away from.

We arrived a few minutes later, and Bosco wrapped his arm around my waist as he escorted me inside.

The man at the podium immediately panicked when

he saw him. "We can get the restaurant cleared out, sir. Just give us—"

"Not necessary," Bosco said as he kept me into his side. "At the lady's request."

"Oh…" The host clearly never expected Bosco to ask for anything else. He grabbed two menus and escorted us to a private table that was spaced noticeably farther away from the other patrons. With a low-burning candle and a small vase of roses, it was a romantic scene.

Like a gentleman, Bosco helped me into my chair before he sat down. The waiter appeared out of thin air, and Bosco ordered a bottle of wine for us to share.

I recognized it right away because it was a bottle my family produced. "You like Barsetti wine?"

"Yes." He glanced at his menu before he met my gaze. "They make fine wine."

"I hope you aren't saying that to impress me."

"Not at all," he said. "You've made it very clear what impresses you."

"Which is?" I asked, interested in his answer.

He wore a serious expression, his blue eyes painfully beautiful. "Nothing."

Unsure what to say, I continued to stare at him.

"A woman who doesn't need anything is impossible to impress—and that's why I like you." He leaned forward with his elbows on the table, infusing me with his presence like he was right beside me. He ignored everyone else in the restaurant even though I saw a few beautiful women look at him. Undeniably handsome, he had dark hair that complemented his tanned skin, and his shoulders looked even broader in the blazer he wore. The V-neck of his shirt showed the musculature of his chest, a hint of his powerful pectorals under his clothes. He was a tall man with a powerful physique, so he attracted the attention of every woman in the room—including mine. "The Barsetti name is a respectable one, even in my world."

"I'm glad to hear that…I guess."

"I know your father and uncle retired to a quiet life decades ago, before I was even born, but I've heard tales of their brutality and strength. I suspect your family is one of the reasons Bones retired, because he was never the kind of man I expected to retire. He's too good at what he does—and he loves money too much."

"All that changed when he met someone he loved more than money—my cousin."

"Must be an exceptional woman."

The waiter returned with the bottle and poured two glasses. Then he took our order and walked away again.

Bosco kept looking at me, like he wanted me to respond to what he'd said.

"She is. We're a lot alike. I feel like we're sisters more than cousins."

"That explains a lot. Barsetti women seem to have a special quality."

"It's all Barsettis," I said proudly, knowing we were a tight-knit family that understood loyalty more than anyone else.

The corner of his mouth rose in a smile. "I like a woman with pride. Another sexy quality."

"Why don't you tell me about your family?" It was the first time I'd asked him a personal question.

His eyes slightly softened like he appreciated the question. "My mother passed away five years ago. Cancer."

"I'm sorry." It was one of the worst ways to go, and I pitied anyone who had to go through it.

He nodded. "It was rough. I was really close to her. So was my brother, Ronan."

"What about your father?"

"That asshole took off after Ronan was born. Decided being a father wasn't his strength, so he abandoned us. I was raised by a single mother, and let me tell you, she did one hell of a job. Worked two jobs to support us, and she got us into the best schools and gave us the best life she could."

I liked the way he spoke about his mother, the same pride in his voice as there was in mine. "You never heard from your father again?"

"No. He'd be stupid to show his face. I'd shoot him right in the stomach and watch him bleed out and die."

I grabbed my glass and gripped it, slightly stunned by easily those words rolled off his tongue.

"I'm not angry at him for leaving. Ronan and I were fine without a father. Our mother played both roles, and she did it a lot better than he ever could. My hatred is on my mother's behalf. I hate him for abandoning her, for knocking her up and leaving her stranded. That's why he deserves to die. I know I had a better life without him around. My mother was the one who had to struggle, not me."

He'd now said something else that surprised me, something that touched my heart. "It sounds like you really loved her." It made sense that he ended up the way he did, a criminal because his life hadn't been perfect the way mine had been.

"I did. Miss her every day." He drank his wine then licked his lips. "I started making serious money in my early twenties. That's when I told her to quit working and relax a bit. Ronan and I put her in a nice apartment here in Florence along with an allowance. She said those years were some of her best. She even had a boyfriend."

"That's really sweet." It was rare to hear about someone who supported their parents. I couldn't imagine doing that for mine since they were well-off. But I knew if something horrible happened, Carter and I would do whatever it took to be there for them. "Did she know what you did for a living?"

He nodded. "Yes."

And she was okay with him breaking the law? Hurting people?

Like he could read my mind, he addressed my thoughts. "Good and evil aren't black and white. You do what you have to do to survive, and I won't apologize or make excuses for my choices. I break the law every day, but I have no regrets."

I still didn't understand exactly what he did because I never asked. After what Griffin told me, I didn't want to know. "And what exactly do you do?"

He watched me for a long time, his eyes serious as he considered his response. It was a question I'd refused to ask, so he never had a chance to answer it. But now, I'd finally asked for the information I'd been dreading receiving. "When Bones told you I control all the money in the city, that was a good way to put it. That's exactly what I do."

"Could you clarify?"

"I run the biggest illegal casino in Italy. It's right here in Florence. Villains and criminals pay their million-dollar memberships to join. Anyone who crosses me or my casino in any way is thrown into the ring."

I'd heard him use that term before. "The ring?"

"It's where we have the Brawl. Two men are put in the center, and all the members bet on who's going to win. It's the biggest highlight of the casino, where most of the cash is made and dealt."

"So they just fight until one gives up?"

He shook his head slightly, a sinister look in his eyes.

That answered my unspoken question.

"They fight to the death," he said out loud. "Winner lives to tell the tale."

Jesus Christ. "And you're in charge of all that?"

He nodded. "Yes. My brother and I do it together."

I didn't know what to say to that. It wasn't as bad as I thought it would be, but it also wasn't good either. On a nightly basis, he saw men die for their crimes. They operated above the law, disregarding it completely. Bosco clearly had immense power, to make two grown men fight like animals for survival.

He continued to watch me, expecting some kind of reaction from me.

I didn't know what reaction I wanted to give. Griffin used to be a hitman before he retired for Vanessa. In some ways, this wasn't nearly as bad. But in other ways, it was worse. "I don't know what to say..."

"It's okay if you have nothing to say. It is what it is."

I drank the rest of my wine and refilled it. He said that he specifically only ran this casino for criminals, so regular men didn't participate. That meant he was constantly surrounded by thugs and hitmen, people just like Griffin. "Is that why you're escorted everywhere you go? Because men want to hurt you?"

"Not necessarily," he said. "It's mostly a sign of power. For people to fear you, you always have to give them a reason to. I have eyes and ears everywhere. There's nothing that happens in my casino or in my life that I don't know about."

"So in the alleyway..."

"They're members of my casino. And when I give an order, they obey it. Otherwise, they'll lose their membership, or worse, they'll be thrown into the ring and forced to fight for their right to take another breath."

"I see..." This man had more power than even Griffin did. "And helping people like me isn't something you're interested in?" My brother and cousin both worked to liberate innocent women who were captured. But Bosco walked by and didn't seem to care that I needed help.

"No." He didn't show me a hint of remorse. "I'm not that kind of guy. I'm not a hero, and I'm not looking to be one. In this life, if you want to survive, you have to watch every step you take. It doesn't matter if you're a man, a woman, or a dog. You have to watch your back as well as your front. You failed to do that—and that's why you needed me there."

I wasn't angry by the answer because he'd been transparent about his motivations from the beginning. He never pretended to be something he wasn't, and even if he wasn't a good guy, at least he was honest.

"But I'm glad that I saved you. Best decision I ever made."

My eyes moved back to his face, seeing the sincerity written in his blue eyes. "Good thing you owed Griffin a favor."

"Yes. Thankfully. But a part of me suspects I would have saved you anyway."

"Why?" I asked, staring into his soft eyes.

"I've never seen a woman put up a fight like that. They just cry and scream. You didn't give up. You held on to your dignity even when you were compromised. It didn't matter that you were outnumbered. You weren't going to stop until you were free. I respect that."

I was flattered by the compliment when I shouldn't be. Anyone else would have done the same thing. To assume a woman would just cry and give up was incorrect. Women were made of more strength than that. "Why did you owe him a favor anyway?" I asked, referring to Griffin.

"One of my dealers filled his pockets on his shift then took off with a few million. Bones is the best in the business, so I hired him to retrieve the dealer. Instead of monetary compensation, Bones asked for a favor debt."

"What's that?" I asked. "A favor debt?"

"It means he can ask me for anything at any time. That's what makes Bones so unique. He works for loyalty as well as money, and that's why it's so easy for him to gain the intel he needs and also to operate in complete secrecy—because no one will rat him out. So when you said he was family in the alleyway, I was obligated to intervene."

Now I was eternally grateful that Griffin asked for loyalty instead of money for some of his jobs. I didn't want to think what would have happened if I didn't have that trick up my sleeve. I would have kept fighting, but there was a good possibility I wouldn't have gotten away. I may have ended up... I didn't even want to think about it.

Bosco's eyes were trained on my face, as if there were words popping up on my cheeks and he was reading them like a book. He examined me with a powerful stare, ignoring the wine on the table because he was focused on me so intensely. "I can keep you safe, Beautiful. With me, you never have to be afraid ever again. You can walk the streets alone naked, and no one will look twice at you—because they know you're mine."

"I never said I was afraid."

"No." He tilted his head slightly. "I'm a great poker player. Probably the best in Italy. I can read people extremely well, regardless of how hard they try to hide their insecurities. I know you're a strong woman who will hold her head high even when she's outnumbered— something I respect you for. But I can also tell that you're frightened, that experience shook you to your core, made you realize how vulnerable you really are. If Bones hadn't been a part of your life, where would you be right now? It's a terrifying thought—and you should be scared."

I held his gaze with the same resolution, but inside, I felt the tremors around my heart. Fear wasn't something I admitted easily, but when he cornered me like that, I couldn't deny it. I had had a few nightmares because of the ordeal, even though I pretended I was perfectly fine when I spoke to Vanessa and Griffin. I didn't take a taxi home every night because I wanted to make Griffin happy. I did it because I was afraid to walk alone in the dark.

Bosco didn't celebrate his victory. "You never have to be scared with me. You'd be invincible. Untouchable." He slowly reached his hand across the table until his fingertips rested on mine. "As the woman on my arm, you'd be the second most powerful person in this city."

"And what do you ask for in exchange?" I asked, knowing the answer before he even gave it.

He brought my hand to his lips and kissed the back of my palm. "You."

WE GOT INTO THE BACK SEAT OF HIS CAR AND GOT ON the road.

I immediately knew he wasn't taking me home because we were going in the opposite direction. We passed the shops and cafes as we headed to the west side of the city, the buildings that had perfect views of the hillsides of Tuscany.

He sat beside me in the back seat of the car, his large hand on my thigh and his fingers poking up my dress slightly. His scent filled the back of the car, cologne mixed with soap, creating a powerful aroma of pure masculinity. He turned his face toward mine and stared at me as we drove through the quiet streets of Florence. It was dark in the back seat, and his chiseled jaw was slightly covered in the shadow. The light from the street hit his eyes perfectly, making them sparkle like diamonds. He was a beautiful man, but some of his best features were hidden in the darkness—just like his soul.

He watched me for minutes, his eyes hardly blinking because he was so absorbed in my features. Now that I'd agreed to give him a chance, he seemed more possessive of me than before. He used to maintain a distance and listen to me, but now those boundaries had been shattered.

I turned my gaze on him and met his gaze fearlessly, refusing to be intimidated by that expression that could soak my panties right off my legs. I watched his eyes slightly shift back and forth as he looked at me, his soft lips surrounded by the dark stubble that was sprinkled on his masculine chin. With a body that dwarfed mine, he was all man, from head to toe, from shoulder to shoulder. "Yes?" I whispered, even though the center divider between the driver and us was closed.

He never gave an answer. Like he hadn't heard me at all, he kept staring at me with the same intensity. His hand moved into my hair, and he cradled my head so he could get a better look at me. His thumb brushed along my bottom lip, but he didn't kiss me. "You're beautiful. From the fierce look in your eyes to your long legs, you're absolutely perfect. I want you underneath me, whispering my name over and over as I make you come. You're a queen, and I'm glad you've given me a chance to be your king."

My breath stopped in my lungs because I was falling under his spell. He said the right things to make me wet, to make my panties slowly sink down my thighs as they became heavier. He was the only man I'd ever met who actually made me feel something, made my thighs squeeze together and pretend my hips were in the center. I realized I was getting deeper into a situation I didn't want to be in, but I couldn't stop myself. I'd always been a logical person, making the right decisions based on reason, not lust and desire. I knew this man was bad for me, but I chose to be with him anyway.

Minutes later, we pulled up to a fifteen-foot gate surrounding a building and passed through until we reached the entryway. With historical architecture but with modern technology, it looked like an impenetrable fortress.

The car pulled up to the front, and the driver opened the back door for Bosco.

Bosco got out first and then helped me out of the car. His arm immediately circled my waist, and we approached the front doors, which were opened for him by two armed men. We walked inside a lobby, where men were gathered in front of monitors that showed the entire perimeter of the building. Two men stood near the elevator, and once pressed the button when we arrived, making the doors open when Bosco approached.

None of them spoke to Bosco. They didn't look at him either. And none of them looked at me.

I held my breath as we passed the two dozen armed men in Bosco's employ. All dressed in black with rifles and pistols, they seemed like they were prepared for war. They all looked the same, with hard expressions and short hair.

I wasn't easily intimidated by anything, but I was certainly uneasy around Bosco's personal army.

When the doors shut and the elevator finally rose, I let the air out of my lungs.

Bosco turned his gaze on me. "No need to be afraid."

"I'm not afraid. I've just never experienced something like that before. Guns have been in my house since I can remember, and I know my father and uncle are familiar with weapons and fighting...but I've never seen anything quite like that. You have a private army."

"In addition to the men who circle the perimeter within a mile radius." He faced forward again, watching the buttons light up as we ascended to the top floor.

"You have a lot of enemies?"

The doors opened, and he stepped inside the penthouse. "If you don't have any enemies, then you're doing something wrong." He took me into his living room, a large space with four couches, an enormous TV, and a private bar. There was a big rustic fireplace and paintings all along the walls.

He immediately stripped off his jacket and hung it on the back of a chair, standing in his fitted t-shirt and jeans. His muscular arms stretched the fabric, and every time he moved, his muscles shifted and changed the way the shirt fit him. He poured two glasses of scotch and handed me one.

I took it, my hand slightly shaking because my heart was still beating fast. This place looked like a penthouse in Manhattan, with stunning views of the city and furniture that was more expensive than a car.

He turned back to the bar and set his watch on the surface, along with his wallet.

I took a long drink to steady my nerves. My family

had always been wealthy, but this was a new level of rich. Bosco was the kind of man that could buy an entire country if he wanted to. He owned his own building along with a private artillery.

He downed his scotch before he came back to me. "Would you like a tour?"

"How big is it?"

"Three floors."

Jesus. "Then I'll pass."

He released a faint chuckle. "Then I'll just show you my bedroom." He took the empty glass out of my hand then grabbed me by the wrist. He must have felt my unsteady heartbeat against his thumb because he said, "Why are you nervous?"

"I'm not nervous."

He brought my wrist to his lips and kissed it, feeling my heartbeat right against my skin. "Your body says otherwise."

"I'm scared...scared of you." If I crossed this man, there would be no escape. My family would be powerless to challenge him. Even Griffin wouldn't be able to help me. This man had more power than any single man should. He had the entire underworld at his disposal, along with a private guard that accompanied him everywhere he went. He had the power and security of a world leader.

He watched me for a long time, slowly lowering my hand back to my side. "You should be. I'm a terrible man who's done terrible things. If you're unfortunate enough to be my enemy, there's no escape." He moved his hand into my hair and tilted my chin so my lips were close to his. "But you never have to be scared of me. I've respected you from the moment I met you. You're the only person in this world who has any power over me."

"I'm just afraid you'll never let me go..." I whispered my darkest fear to him, that I was his prisoner without even realizing it. Now that I was here, I wondered if I really had a choice. If I wanted to walk away, would I be able to? He could kill my entire family to make me cooperate. He could take away everything I loved if I failed to please him.

He lowered his mouth to mine and gave me a soft kiss. "I worry about the same thing." He looked me in the eye before he kissed me again, this time harder. His muscular arm wrapped around my waist, and he pulled me tight against him, making me feel his hard cock in his jeans.

Despite the terror in my heart, I kissed him back, falling victim to the attraction that was impossible to deny. My pulse beat with the rhythm of danger, but that only made me kiss him harder, cling to him out of desperation. My hand fisted his short hair, and I sucked his bottom lip before I gave him my tongue. The only thing that made sense about our relationship was this, this inexplicable passion the likes of which I'd never encountered in my life. Now that I had it, I wanted it desperately; I couldn't live without it. The thought of going back to the average men who barely fit the bill sounded like the most depressing thing in the world.

He kissed me back with the same aggression, nearly swallowing me whole. He guided me backward as he yanked my dress over my ass and bunched it around my waist. His hands gripped my ass cheeks hard before he smacked them both.

I yanked his shirt off then circled my arms around his neck, letting him pull me up and wrap me around his waist. My clit met his cock through his jeans, and our bodies throbbed together, aching to be connected skin to skin.

He carried me past the windows and into his bedroom at the corner of the penthouse. Enormous, with floor-to-ceiling windows and a breathtaking view of the lights of the city, it was a view only a king could have. He set me on the bed and dropped his jeans and boxers, getting naked as quickly as possible. His cock came free, thick and pulsating. His head was slightly dark from all the blood rushing there. It twitched when I stared right at it, my tongue swiping across my bottom lip.

His eyes darkened noticeably. "Get that damn dress off."

I unzipped the back to the top of my waist and let it fall apart, revealing my bare tits. There were pieces of tape over both of them so my nipples wouldn't show.

He gripped stripes of tape with his fingers and ripped them off quickly, making me scream slightly at the abrasion. Then he pushed me down on the bed so he could suck my tits raw, make them even more sensitive than they already were. His tongue gently dragged over my skin, making up for the savage way he'd kissed me a moment ago. Back and forth he went, from being hostile to being loving.

He grabbed the bunched-up material around my waist and yanked it off, pulling it down my longs legs and taking my heels as he went. He moved for my thong last, leaving me completely naked on his bed.

I was the kind of woman that waxed, so my body was always in tip-top shape. I loved the way he looked at me, like he'd never seen a sexier woman in all his life. There must have been hundreds of gorgeous women before me, but like they didn't matter, I was the only one he was thinking about.

We'd done it missionary the last two times we'd had sex, so I turned over and arched my back, showing him the prominent curves of my ass. I let him look at me from a new angle, seeing me in a way he never had before.

His knees sank into the mattress behind me, and then his large hands moved over my cheeks, his thumb swiping across my asshole. "Fucking perfect." His hands moved up my back to the back of my neck. He squeezed me harshly before he pressed his mouth to my slit and kissed me.

Kissed me good.

I closed my eyes and moaned, loving the aggressive way he ignited me instantly. It was rare for a man to have the balls to handle my cunt with his mouth, and Bosco didn't hesitate for a second.

He pulled his mouth away and moved up my arched body, kissing my other entrance.

I moaned unexpectedly, shocked that Bosco would move to that territory next. I gripped the sheets underneath me, enjoying it but also feeling disturbed at the exact same time.

"Every inch of you, from your mouth, to your pussy, to your ass, is fucking perfect." He shifted back to the balls of his feet then abruptly turned me over, rolling me to my back with my head on his pillow.

He moved on top of me, separating my thighs with his and pressing his throbbing cock against my wet pussy. His pretty eyes locked on mine, and he slowly ground against me, stimulating my clit with his impressive thickness.

My hands moved over his chest, and I officially stopped thinking about anything remotely logical. All I thought about was this beautiful man and letting him have me. I wanted him to take all of me, to put me on his list of best women he'd fucked. I wanted to mark this bed with my shape, to leave my scent on the sheets so he would remember me when I was gone. I wanted to come around his dick over and over and not care what happened the following morning.

He settled on top of me and then rubbed his nose against mine. "You look even more beautiful in my bed."

"More beautiful than all the others?" I whispered, my hand exploring the muscles of his shoulder.

He kissed the corner of my mouth. "No contest." He kissed the other corner. "And I knew you were jealous."

"Is this where you fucked that other woman?" One of the things I liked most about Bosco was his complete honesty. He gave truthful answers, even if you didn't want to hear them. It was refreshing compared to the bullshit excuses other men made.

"Yes. Right here." He continued to grind against me. "This is where I fucked her and wished she were you." He kissed me, sucking my bottom lip into his mouth. "The moment I realized I needed to get you in this bed and never let you leave. The moment I knew I only wanted you." He sucked my bottom lip again before he looked me in the eye, his eyes filled with lust and longing.

Those words shouldn't have made me soften, but they did. I felt my body relax into his sheets, felt my heart fill with more longing. His words weren't some line to get me on my back, and that meant something to me. I wasn't jealous of the woman he had just fucked days ago. If anything, she was jealous of me.

"I love looking at you as I fuck you. You're too beautiful not to look at." He pointed his cock at my entrance and slowly slid inside.

It felt so good at the moment that I almost didn't stop him. Skin-to-skin with so much arousal between us, he felt like a godsend. He stretched me even better, my soft flesh enveloping his hardness perfectly. It was so good, my nails sliced his skin.

But then I found the strength to resist. "Condom."

He held himself on top of me, his eyes narrowed on my face. "No." He sank a little deeper.

I bit my bottom lip because it felt so right, so good I actually moaned. "Put on a condom, or nothing happens." This time, I pushed him in the chest, forcing him not to go any deeper. He was using my arousal against me to get what he wanted, but I wouldn't let that happen. "Now." I pushed on his hips, forcing his big dick out of me.

He reached for the nightstand and grabbed a piece of paper instead of a condom. He handed it to me as he stared down at me, waiting for me to read it.

"What the hell is this?"

"I'm clean. Just got tested yesterday."

I narrowed my eyes and confirmed the date and the information.

He took the paper back and tossed it on the floor. "I don't need your papers. I trust you." He pushed inside me again.

"Whoa." I pressed my hand against his chest, keeping him from diving deep inside me. "Just because we're clean doesn't mean that's gonna happen. The only time condoms aren't used is when—"

"We're monogamous. I only fuck you, and you only fuck me." He thrust his hips hard, pushing himself deep inside me with a single motion. He pushed through my warm flesh and entered me completely, stretching me wide apart.

I gripped his shoulders and moaned loudly when I felt him, his cock feeling so damn good I couldn't even think straight. I was so wet, and he was so hard. Feeling him bare was so much better than the latex that separated us. I loved feeling his warm flesh, the distinct hardness of his girth. I loved feeling him in such a deeper way, so intimate, in a way I'd never felt a man before.

"You're mine." He wrapped his hand around my throat without squeezing me. With a slight hint of rage in his eyes, he possessed me in every way imaginable. He took me in a way a man never had before. Buried deep inside me with a girth no other man could compare to, he was a man who conquered the unconquerable. "And I am yours." He thrust into me deep and hard, sliding through my slickness and pushing through my tightness. He made me feel like a virgin, like he was breaking me in all over again. His cock stretched me deeper than any other man had before, making me clutch him so tightly it seemed like I would never let him go.

I moaned in his face as he shook my body back and forth. "Bosco..."

"Beautiful." He watched me as he fucked me, his powerful body tightening and shifting with his movements.

"Fuck me." My hands dug into his hair, and I widened my legs so he could take me, stake his claim all over me. I'd never let a man inside me like this, and now

I was glad I'd waited so long. Bosco was the only man who had earned it, had fucked me good enough to feel my bare pussy. "Take me."

His eyes darkened even more, and his jaw clenched like he was furious. My words turned him on so much, he wasn't sure how to handle it. He rocked his hips harder, hitting me at a deeper angle so he ground against my clit at the same time.

"Yes..." I grabbed his ass and dragged him harder into me. "Like that..."

"This pussy is mine." He smacked his headboard into the wall, making it clap loudly and release a thunderous noise.

"Yes. Yours." My head rolled back as I felt the fire burn in my belly. It grew bigger and bigger, starting from a small kindling and turning into a raging inferno. It burned me from the inside out, and then I came with a scream, yanking him deep inside me as I came all over his dick. Skin on skin, I dumped my arousal all over his length, soaking him down to his balls. "Bosco." My arm wrapped around his neck, and I held on to him as I finished, getting cramps in both feet because my toes curled so much.

"Shit." He kept fucking me, pressing me farther into the mattress because he was moving at such tremendous speed. He fucked me harder than any other man had, pounding into me with the endurance of a racehorse. He clenched his jaw and remained in control, hitting me deep and forcefully without hitting his trigger.

I wanted to come again, but seeing the sexy way his sweat coated his muscles and the strained cords in his neck made me want to see him dive over the cliff, see him lose himself in me the way I lost myself in him. "Bosco...come inside me." I grabbed his hips and guided him inside me, slowing him down as my eyes focused on his.

He released a deep breath, like he'd been holding it for minutes. His eyes darted back and forth between mine, and he thickened slightly inside me. "You want to feel my come inside you, Beautiful?"

"Yes...please."

He clenched his jaw and groaned. "Fuck." He gave his final pumps then shoved himself completely inside me, releasing with a moan so loud, it echoed off the walls. He pressed his forehead against mine as he emptied himself, stuffing my pussy with every single drop of his come. "Jesus Christ..." Seconds later, he started to soften, his warm come sitting deep inside my cunt. He pulled his head away and looked me in the eye, satisfied but aroused at the same time. "You're gonna have so much come sitting inside, you'll feel it for a week."

I cupped his face and kissed him, feeling his softening length inside me. "Can I get that in writing?"

IT WAS TWO IN THE MORNING WHEN WE FINALLY DRIFTED off to sleep.

He spooned me from behind, his powerful chest pressed against my back and his thick arm wrapped around my waist. Every time he took a breath, I felt it drift across the back of my neck and through my hair. He was still sweaty from all the fucking, his heat chasing away any hint of winter.

It would be so easy for me to lie there until morning, but I had work to do and I didn't want to stay over. Sleepovers felt too romantic, and while we had a deeper relationship than before, I didn't want it to get more serious than that.

I gently moved from under his arm and scooted to the edge of the bed.

He didn't move, but his powerful voice filled the quiet space of his bedroom. "If you think you're going home tonight, you're wrong. Get your ass over here now."

I froze in place, a little terrified by the anger in his voice. "I have to work in the morning."

"You think I give a damn?" He sat up and held me by the wrist. Aggressively, he yanked me back toward him, having strength that outmatched a bear. When he had me back in the center of the bed, he looked down at me, still just as angry as before. "I'll make sure you get to work on time." He lay down again, sighing in frustration at my attempt to leave. "Don't pull that stunt again. It's impossible to get in and out of this penthouse without the code—so don't bother."

"So, I'm trapped?" I asked.

"You're trapped with the most powerful man in this country." He moved on top of me and looked down at me like he despised me. "The only thing you should be doing is sleeping soundly, knowing there's not a damn thing out there that could ever hurt you." He lay down again, this time staying on his side of the bed without touching me. His affection died the second I pissed him off. Now, he was stuck on the other side of the bed, taking his warmth and leaving me in the cold.

I wasn't comfortable anymore.

One arm rested behind his head while the other lay on his stomach. He lay still as he stared at the ceiling. "Why are you like that?"

"Like what?" I whispered.

"You don't like to sleep with men."

I shrugged. "I've been sleeping alone my whole life. I don't like to share my space. I don't like to alter my routine."

"That's gonna change." He closed his eyes and turned his head the other way, facing the large window that overlooked the city.

I'd wanted to leave a moment ago, but that was an instinctual decision. I was used to doing the walk of shame or kicking dates out of my apartment the second I was done. I liked going back to my single life the second I knew the man wasn't the right one for me. Now that I was in a different situation, I wasn't sure what to do. All I knew was, I was a lot more comfortable when I had this man wrapped around me, keeping me warm and comfortable. Now, he was pissed at me, insulted by the way I'd tried to creep out of his apartment and past the army waiting at the bottom of the elevator.

After a few minutes of discomfort, I scooted closer to him and rested my face against his shoulder. My arm hooked around his waist, and I tucked my leg between his, snuggling with him like he was my full-time lover. The second I was in place, I felt a million times more comfortable.

His deep voice broke the silence again. "That's better."

8

BOSCO

W<small>HEN</small> I <small>WOKE</small> up the next morning, Carmen was exactly where I left her.

All over me.

Her hand rested against my chest, her face cradled in my shoulder. She had her gorgeous leg draped across my body, and her long hair was soft against my arm. She was dead asleep, sleeping peacefully despite her pathetic attempt to disappear in the middle of the night.

Like I would let that happen.

I didn't do sleepovers either. My dates were sent home in a private car with an escort so I wouldn't feel like such an asshole. But having Carmen there was a different story. I expected her to sleep with me all through the night. I told her she was mine—and she was mine in every sense of the word.

I rolled her over onto her back and watched her eyes slowly open to take me in. Her green eyes were even more beautiful in the morning, despite her smeared mascara and eyeliner. Her lipstick was long gone, probably all over my body. I positioned one of her knees over my shoulder to widen her legs so I could slip my fat dick inside her.

That woke her up.

Her hands immediately went to my arms, and she gripped me tightly as she felt my big dick stretch her wide apart. She panted in my face and moaned as I rocked into her, giving it to her nice and slow, unlike last night. She was still full of my come, but I would give her more before we both started our day.

Her hands moved through my hair, and she moaned quietly for me, enjoying the slow pace I used. She loved my cock, and it was impossible to hide, especially after the performance she gave last night. She was two different people sometimes. She put up a front, pretending she was indifferent to me, but when we were together like this, there was no hiding how she truly felt.

She was crazy about me.

I'd assumed some asshole broke her heart so it was impossible for her to trust someone again. But since that wasn't the case, I knew she was so content being alone that she didn't want to risk getting her heart broken. Unless it was a safe bet, she wouldn't take it.

I wasn't a safe bet.

I couldn't blame her. I wasn't exactly the kind of guy to introduce to your mom.

But we would never get that far anyway. This was just

an intense fling, a monogamous relationship until the fire burned out. I'd never been this intimate with a woman, preferring to have random hookups with women whose names I wouldn't remember. I'd never been with the same woman twice—until Carmen. Now I was doing something new, committing to a woman for a period of time. All I knew was I wanted her and didn't want anyone else to have her. I wanted to enjoy her fully, come deep inside her, and fill her with my come. I wanted to take her out to dinner and show her off. I wanted to take her to my casino so men could hate me even more than they already did. I wanted to treasure her as mine and mine alone.

And I wanted to protect her. Make her feel like a queen. Make her come so hard that she would never want another man except me.

It seemed like my plan was working.

I screwed her nice and slow, waking her up in the most sensual way possible. I rubbed her clit just how she liked and made her come around my dick, made her sink into my mattress as I took her exactly as I wanted.

And she gave herself to me.

She moaned in my face and squeezed her thighs against my hips, bucking slightly in pleasure. "Bosco...yes."

My name had never sounded sexier

I'd been hard since I woke up, so I gave her a few pumps before I released inside her, making another deposit into the pussy I now owned. I gave her every single drop, my spine shivering at the same time. There was nothing better than coming deep inside a woman. This was my first time—and it was better than I'd ever imagined.

I rolled off her then glanced at the time on the clock on my nightstand. We both got off in less than five minutes.

She was an easy woman to please.

I got out of bed then pulled on my boxers and sweatpants.

She lay there, her body still and her eyes closed like she was ready to go back to sleep.

"I'll have breakfast ready in ten minutes." I walked into the kitchen and got the pans going, preparing two slices of salmon and a side of greens. My diet was just as strict as my exercise regimen. I worked out hard every day in my private gym, and I avoided carbs like they were poison. My habits got me into this perfect form, so it wasn't difficult for me to remain disciplined. Since Carmen had a perfect figure, I assumed she was a picky eater as well.

She walked into the kitchen, her hair messy and her eyes still tired from the climax she'd just had. But what was most surprising of all was what she was wearing.

My shirt.

I turned away from the stove and stared at her, barely able to believe what I was actually looking at. This was the woman who kicked me out the second I rolled the condom off. She was the one who tried to sneak out last night. But now she wearing my t-shirt better than I ever had. It was baggy on her slender body, but far sexier than the sluttiest lingerie. I kept staring at her because I couldn't stop.

She grabbed the coffeepot and poured herself a cup, dismissing my stare because she was probably used to it. "What smells so good?"

I turned back to the stove and turned off the burners. "Salmon and asparagus."

"For breakfast?" she asked incredulously. "Where are the pancakes?"

I couldn't tell if she was being serious or not. "I don't eat pancakes." I grabbed two plates and transferred the food. I carried it to the dining table along with my cup of coffee.

Looking like the sexiest thing in the world, she sat across from me and sipped her coffee again, the shirt the size of a blanket on her petite frame. She grabbed her fork and took a bite. "Wow...this is pretty good."

I ate quietly, more interested in looking at her than talking to her.

"You eat this every day?"

I nodded.

"It's good, but it seems like something you would eat for dinner."

"I suppose. What do you eat for breakfast?" I had no idea since she always kicked me out.

"Nothing, actually. I'm usually in a hurry to get out the door. But when I do eat breakfast, it's always pancakes. You know, pancakes with fruit, nuts, tons of syrup..."

"You make it sound like a sundae."

"Yeah, it kinda is. And it's delicious."

I could never eat anything like that. I needed protein to keep my muscles strong, and I couldn't have any carbs in order to keep my ripped physique. I was all muscle and no fat. That was exactly the way the ladies liked me.

"Are you going to work this morning?" she asked.

"No. I work out in the mornings. I don't head to the casino until the afternoon."

"Where do you work out?"

"The second floor. I have a gym."

"Of course you do." She looked around my apartment, admiring the fine furniture and the beautiful paintings on the wall. My place was designed with refinement and masculinity, dark colors mixed with tones of gray and white. She finished her food then took both of our plates. "I'll do the dishes since you cooked."

"Leave them in the sink," I ordered. "My maid will take care of it."

"Your maid?" She turned around after putting the dishes in the sink, having listened to me and probably understanding what would happen if she disobeyed. "Does she live here?"

"No. She comes when I'm at the gym. Does the dishes, handles my laundry, changes the sheets on my bed...stuff like that."

"I'm surprised you give anyone the code to this place."

"She gets a new one ten minutes before her shift starts."

A slight look of surprise came onto her face, but she covered it up quickly. "Well, I should get going..." She leaned against the counter and gripped the edge, but she didn't move back toward the bedroom to change. She seemed to linger, like she wasn't sure if she really wanted to go or not.

I moved toward her until I had her back perfectly pressed into the counter. My hands gripped the edge on either side of her so I had her blocked in with nowhere to go. My mouth hovered inches from hers, my blue eyes looking into her beautiful green ones. I'd just fucked her in my bed, and now I wanted to do it again. This woman did crazy things to me. Those long legs drove me wild, and those full lips made me feel like a teenage boy all over again. "How do you feel?" I loved pumping my come inside her, loved owning her in a way no other man had. The idea of being with another woman nearly disgusted me because Carmen was all I wanted—the perfect fit.

"Full." She gave the perfect answer, her eyes dancing playfully as she said it. She tried to fight the smile on her lips, but it was no use. She was practically grinning, happy and satisfied from our night together.

I kissed her, my mouth anxious to worship hers. She gave me her tongue right away, and I took it with greed, wanting everything this woman was willing to give me. She made me want to be a better man, but she also brought out my worst qualities. If she really wanted to move on from me, I wasn't sure if I could let her go. I might capture her straight from her apartment and make her into my prisoner. If she refused to cooperate, I would execute every single member of her family. I'd never wanted a woman as much as I wanted her, and if I didn't get what I wanted, there was no telling what might happen.

It was a scary thought.

Not for me. But for her.

She ended the kiss by gently pushing on my chest. "I should head home. I have a lot to do at the shop today."

I had a pair of handcuffs in my drawer, and I was tempted to chain her to the headboard so she could only leave when I was ready for her to. But that seemed excessive, especially when I had a busy schedule. "Alright. Get dressed, and one of my men will take you." She had no idea how sinister my thoughts were, how much she turned me into a monster. She had every reason to be scared.

She was smart to be scared.

Despite Ronan's objections, I took The Butcher's money and gave him a membership to the casino. He fit in with everyone else, but he also stuck out like a sore thumb. He was loud, obnoxious, and unpredictable, and it was easy to tell if he was in the casino at any given time.

I walked around the floor, seeing all the men playing at the poker tables while the girls danced on their poles and in cages at random spots throughout the floor. Music played overhead, smoke from cigars rose to the ceiling, and there was so much testosterone in one place, it seemed like it might explode.

I wore one of my best suits, watching my kingdom as I ruled from my perch. Cameras were everywhere, along with security guards. Unlike other casinos, all the security teams wore guns, while the patrons weren't allowed to bring weapons at all.

Ronan came to my side, dressed in a black suit and matching tie. "I've gotten nothing but complaints about him."

"What kind of complaints?" I stared down at all the tables from the balcony, watching the men wear their best poker faces.

"The dancers tell me he gropes them every chance he gets."

"That's not unusual."

"Tried to rape one of them in the bathroom."

Alright...that was a little too far. "Give him a warning. He has two more. Otherwise, he'll be banned from the casino." I couldn't throw him into the ring unless he actually stole from the casino.

"Some of the best girls already quit." Ronan didn't

hide his annoyance. He hated the decision I made and would look for any reason to prove I'd made the wrong call.

"Tell them it won't happen again and offer them a raise."

He shook his head slightly. "The only reason why we have the best girls is because they feel safe here. If we fuck that up, we'll be stuck with the hags."

"Which is why you need to assure them it won't happen again."

"Then you need to warn The Butcher. He doesn't listen to me." He pivoted his body toward me, his hands in the pockets of his suit. "It'll be better coming from you."

"Alright." I pulled a cigar out of my pocket and lit it. Smoke drifted to the ceiling, and I took a drag on the end, bringing the smoke into my lungs. I let everything out through my nose and mouth at the same time. "I'll take care of it."

"Good." He relaxed now that the conversation was over. "What's new with you?" Whenever we finished talking about business, we had our personal relationship, the same kind of relationship all brothers had.

"Nothing." I didn't tell him about Carmen because I wasn't sure what to say. It was the first time I'd been obsessed with pussy, and I didn't know what that meant. I couldn't figure out if I wanted to keep her as a pet or adore her as a woman. "You?"

"Saw flowers at Mother's grave. I'm guessing that was you."

"Yes." I went to her grave pretty often, not just on her birthday and the anniversary of her death. My mother had been the biggest role model in my life. She'd taught me how to be a man, raised me to be strong, smart, and intuitive. She didn't take shit from anybody, and she never refrained from giving me the beating of a lifetime if I deserved it. Carmen's fiery attitude reminded me of my mother's spirit sometimes. Perhaps that was the real reason why I helped her in that alleyway...and I'd been obsessed with her ever since. "What's new with you?"

"I've been fucking Giada."

Giada was one of the dancers on the floor. Ronan seemed to rotate through the girls. Whenever we had new women working for us, he made his move and screwed them for a while before he moved on to the next one. "Pretty girl."

"Yeah. She's flexible."

I chuckled before I took another drag. "Well, dancers tend to be." I usually mentioned the women I was fucking to Ronan, but only because we were family. We didn't exchange other personal information, like our thoughts, stresses, and feelings. We'd never been that way. But we could talk about sex...because we both liked sex.

Ronan placed his hand on my shoulder before he walked away. "I'll bring The Butcher to your office. Good luck."

"Thanks." I inhaled from the cigar again. "But I'm not gonna need it."

———

THE BUTCHER WAS A LARGE MAN, BUILT LIKE A BRICK shithouse the way Bones was. He had an extra twenty pounds of muscle on his frame than I did, but that didn't make him intimidating. As my brother described it, his unpredictability was the worst part of his character.

My fortune was based on reading people, guessing their next move before they made it. Interacting with a man like The Butcher wasn't my forte, not when his thoughts were locked away behind a ten-foot gate.

Ronan escorted him to my office and motioned for him to take a seat in the leather armchair.

I let my lit cigar sit in the ashtray, the smoke slowly rising up to the ceiling. I wasn't a big smoker, only on occasion. But today seemed like a good day to light up, especially when I was dealing with a psychopath who was already shaking up my casino.

He stared at me, a crooked grin on his face. His smile wasn't strong enough to distract from the scars all over his face. He had cuts from a blade along his forehead, his cheeks, and his chin. Perfectly spaced out, the marks clearly had been made on purpose, and the scars were so noticeable that it was obvious the cuts had been deep. He tilted his head from the left to the right as his narrowed his eyes on me. "Uh-oh. The boss." He chuckled, seeing this as some kind of twisted game. "The second your little bitch touched me on the shoulder, I knew I was in trouble."

"Or you knew you were in trouble because you tried to rape one of my dancers."

He shrugged. "Just tried to stick it in her ass a little."

I kept a straight face, not amused by the comment at all. "The dancers are off-limits, Butcher. Bother any of them again, and I'll have you banned from the casino. It's a bit pathetic that you've been a member for a week, but you're already about to be kicked out."

"You laid out the rules perfectly clear—and you didn't mention a damn thing about the dancers."

"It's implied," I said coldly. "Don't harass, assault, or touch any of my girls."

"I guess I don't see the girls as people," he said with a shrug. "Just asses and tits."

I'd never been a gentleman or the type of man to defend a woman, but his attitude rubbed me the wrong way. I might not go out of my way to protect a woman, but I'd certainly never considered raping or hurting one. Only a true psychopath thought that way. "Well, the girls here are a different story. Step out of line again, and I'll have to remove you. Just gamble, make some money, and go home. It's not that hard."

"Or lose some money," he said with a laugh. "That's how you make your cash, right?"

"I gamble as well."

"What's your game?" He kept turning his head, like a bird that couldn't sit still.

"Poker."

He nodded slowly. "I'll have to play you sometime. Wipe you out."

"I'm up for the challenge. Assuming you're still a member in the next week."

He grinned a little too hard. "Alright, boss. I'll be on my best behavior. I guess I'll have to get my urges out elsewhere."

I didn't agree with his statement since it felt morally wrong to encourage a man to harass women like that. It made me sick to my stomach, not that I should care what he did or who he did it to. "Strike one, Butcher. There better not be a strike two."

My men secured a perimeter with a three-mile radius, and I walked past the windows of the flower shop before I stepped inside. It'd been a few days since I'd spoken to Carmen. I'd been busy with work—and with The Butcher.

Carmen must have been in the back room because no one was in the store. I admired the arrangements she had on display and looked at the pictures she had on the wall. There was a calendar next to the register, and feminine handwriting was scribbled everywhere, dates she had to remember for specific events.

I was in jeans and a gray hoodie, dressed casually on this cold winter day. It was overcast because of the thick clouds, and it looked like it might rain. Tomorrow was Saturday, and I hoped I'd be spending the weekend in between Carmen's legs.

She emerged from the back room, wearing skintight dark jeans, brown boots, and a dark blue sweater that fit the beautiful curves of her body. Her hair was in loose curls as it trailed past her tits to her stomach. She had exceptionally long hair, perfect for fisting when we were in bed together. She looked up to address me, clearly in a good mood because she was doing what she loved for a living. But when she realized it was me, all that happiness instantly vanished from her face.

"You don't look happy to see me." I stood at the counter and stared her down, a smile on my lips but not in my voice. When she left my penthouse the other day, she kissed me hard on the mouth and reluctantly left my shirt behind. Now she acted like I'd just ruined her day.

"I just..." She glanced out the window, as if she were afraid someone would see her. "Griffin and Vanessa drop by pretty often, and so does my father. The last thing I want is for any of them to see you."

"Ouch," I said sarcastically.

"Maybe we're sleeping together monogamously and we have some sort of relationship, but my feelings about the situation haven't changed. My father would lose his mind if he ever found out about this. He would tell my uncle, and it would turn into another world war. Trust me on this, I've seen it happen with my own eyes. And Griffin...he'd probably be even worse. So you need to stop dropping by like this."

"You're mine, and I can do whatever I want." I gripped the edge of the counter as I stared her down. I wasn't the kind of man that lived a lie. I was exactly who I wanted to be, and if someone didn't like it, that was their problem.

Her eyes flashed with hostility. "My family means everything to me. They're the single most important thing in my life, and I would rather die than ever hurt them. So if you really want me, you have to accept those terms. You will always be a dirty secret and nothing more. If you can't accept that, then get the hell out of my shop and don't show your face again." Like a fire that started from a single twig, she came to life instantly.

Her fearlessness never failed to surprise me, and I found myself so hard in my jeans I might break through the zipper. Other men dispersed when I walked into a room, intuitively feared me and dropped their gazes out of dread of my hostility, but this woman had no problem telling me off.

She wasn't afraid of me at all, at least not when it came to her family.

Fucking hot.

She kept looking at me with that same rage, like she was prepared to fight me if necessary.

That would be even hotter.

"Just a dirty secret, huh?" I asked. "That sounds pretty hot."

Her shoulders relaxed slightly, and she reached her hand under the counter to do something discreetly. She did a good job of hiding it from me, but nothing could escape my notice.

"I can do that. But don't expect to be my dirty secret." I intended to wear her on my arm, to show the world she was mine—and mine alone.

The phone at the counter started to ring, so she walked away to answer it. "Hello, Carmen's Flowers. How may I help you?" Her back was turned to me as she grabbed the pad and pen to take the order.

I moved behind the counter to see what she'd been hiding.

A gun.

I picked it up and checked the magazine—it was fully loaded.

And the safety was off.

I put it back where it belonged, but I couldn't wipe the smirk off my face. This woman was prepared to shoot me if she had to, to put a bullet right in my chest if I crossed the line. She knew I was lethal and took that seriously, arming herself because that was the only defense she had.

Now I wanted her even more.

I returned to the other side of the counter and pretended I hadn't discovered the gun.

She finished the call and came back to me. "I have a lot of orders this week. A few funerals."

"That's too bad."

"I guess the flu is hitting people pretty hard." She tore off the piece of paper and put it in a pile along with her other orders. She stood right in front of the gun, strategically placing herself in case she needed it.

I'd never wanted a woman more. I couldn't take my eyes off her, finding her courage the sexiest thing in the world. She was willing to do anything to keep her family safe, even go head-to-head with me. She would have to put at least three bullets in me to slow me down because the first two just wouldn't be enough.

She kept her eyes on me, studying me the way I studied her. "Look...I know that came off rude. When Vanessa brought Griffin around, my family refused to accept him. It was a really difficult year, and her parents went through a lot. I understand why she did it because he was the man she loved and wanted to marry. But I'm not gonna put my family through that. My parents don't have to love the guy I want to be with, but they at least have to accept him. If they knew about us..." She rolled her eyes. "My family wouldn't stop until you disappeared. They're very protective of me."

I couldn't blame them, not when she was such a bombshell. She was the most beautiful woman I'd ever seen, independent, smart, and sexy. She was every guy's fantasy—but only my reality. I couldn't blame her father and her uncle for having high standards for the man she chose. I might be rich and successful, but I had more flaws than positive qualities. Not to mention, I was fucking dangerous.

"So don't show up in my shop or at my apartment. You have my phone number—use it."

While I appreciated the calm way she spoke to me, I respected the gun under her counter a lot more. I liked the way she got big and loud when it came to her family. I'd always been the same way about my brother, willing to do anything for him at any time. He was all I had left now, the only person who would always have my back—no matter what. "I'm going to give you some advice."

"Advice?" she asked, surprised by the change in subject.

"Always stand up for what you believe in and never back down—not even to me." I nodded downward, indicating the gun she had stashed away. "Never settle for less than what you deserve. The more respect you earn, the more power you earn—and the safer you'll be."

I TEXTED HER WHEN I GOT INTO THE CAR. *I'M COMING OVER.* I'd been waiting around for her to finish her day at work and head back to her apartment. The second she walked through the door, as my men informed me, I told her what I wanted.

I just walked in the door.

Yes. I know.

I didn't get a response, which told me she was pissed by that answer. *I'll be there in ten minutes.*

I was escorted to her apartment, and I walked up the stairs until I reached her door. Like last time, I snapped through her locks and invited myself inside. "Beautiful, I'm here." I locked the door behind me.

She came down the hallway, in the same outfit she'd been wearing earlier. "Knock."

I raked my eyes over her body as she came close to me, treasuring the sight of her beautiful curves and even more beautiful face.

"You can't just—"

I didn't hear the rest of the sentence because I wrapped my arms around her and kissed her, squeezing her hard against me in the entryway.

Her anger died in her throat, and she kissed me back, forgetting the reason she was pissed in the first place. Her arms locked around my neck, and she kissed me like she'd missed me all day, despite the cold way she spoke to me.

I backed her up against the wall and dug my hand into her curls, loving the way they felt in my fist when I held on to her. I hooked her leg over my hip and breathed into her mouth, feeling her tits through her bra right against my chest. Just because she told me not to come into her shop didn't mean I wouldn't keep an eye on her and make sure no one bothered her. When I told her being with me was the safest place she would ever be, I meant it.

I would protect her—even if I weren't there.

When I pulled away, all the anger she had was gone. She looked at me with the same expression she wore in bed, like I was the one thing that mattered. It was the only time she was soft toward me, when our naked bodies were combined together and our mouths dragged across each other's skin.

The rest of the time, she hated me.

Hated everything I stood for.

I rubbed my nose against hers. "I missed you."

She gave me a light kiss on the corner of my mouth. "I missed you too." Maybe she only meant it in that moment, or maybe she didn't mean it at all, just wanted to repeat the words back to me because of the heat between us.

It didn't matter to me. I just enjoyed listening to her beautiful voice. I lifted her against my chest and carried her to the couch in the living room. I sat back and held her with me, remembering the time we'd fucked in that very spot. Now I just wanted to look at her, wanted to feel this beautiful woman in my arms. "How about I make dinner tonight?"

"You're going to cook for me again?" she asked, cocking her head slightly.

"Yes." My hands rested at her hips, the sexy curve in her perfect body.

"And what are you going to cook?" she asked, her hands rubbing against my chest.

"Whatever you want."

"Hot sex and a home-cooked meal? I'm one lucky lady."

"No." I brought her left hand to my lips and kissed it, keeping my eyes on her. "I'm the lucky one."

Her eyes softened slightly, but she quickly forced the look away, like she was embarrassed for feeling anything in the first place. She had a good poker face, but the longer we spent together, the harder it was to keep it up. The armor she wore was slowly coming undone, and she began to drop her guard, allowing herself to want me. She was still scared of me, sensed the danger in my rough exterior, but she was starting to disregard it. "What have you been doing for the last few days?"

"Checking up on me, huh?" I asked, wondering if she'd thought about me during our two days of silence. So far, I was always the one to contact her. She'd never called me or texted me. She was too proud to do it. But that would change soon enough.

"Just curious."

"I worked at the casino. Gambled a bit."

"Win or lose?"

"I lost a hundred thousand."

She cringed.

"But then won two million."

"Oh, wow...that is a nice casino."

I shrugged. "I'm just a damn good poker player."

"Yeah?" she asked, sitting on my hard-on like it was the perfect seat for her.

"You should watch me play sometime."

"I've played poker a few times."

"Yeah?" The idea of her gambling turned me on. Watching her sit at a table with powerful men and hold her own was sexy as hell. I hooked up with all kinds of women, none of them fitting into a specific category. But my obsession with Carmen told me I found her characteristics particularly attractive, the way she held herself with so much confidence. To my surprise, a strong woman was my weakness. She ran her own business, lived alone, and she didn't cower in the face of a more powerful enemy.

"With Vanessa and our fathers. We just play for fun, but it's a good time."

"Do you clean them out?"

"Oh, always," she said with a laugh. "But they probably let us win."

I'd probably do the same. "Come to the casino with me tomorrow night. You can sit on my arm and watch me play."

All of her playfulness evaporated into thin air. "That's not a good idea."

"And why not?"

"This is just a fling—no public appearances." Regardless of how she melted for me when we were in bed together, she held on to her beliefs. She was determined to keep this relationship as secretive as possible.

"That's a shame." I pulled her slightly toward me, making her move up my length. "I wanted to show you off. Have you wear a beautiful dress with a slit up to here." My hand moved to the top of her thigh, where the skin would be exposed in the fabulous dress.

"I can wear that dress behind closed doors. Then you can take it off me." She held my gaze with a hint of fearlessness, her confidence so unbelievably sexy.

"That's not a terrible compromise." I lifted her sweater until her cleavage was exposed in the bra. I kissed the soft flesh of her beautiful tits, smelling her perfume and tasting her delectable goodness.

She released a sigh at my touch. "You love my rack, don't you?"

"Nicest tits I've ever seen." I cherished the voluptuous curves of her breasts, loving how soft they were against my tongue. "And I've seen a lot of tits." I saw them every day at the casino as the women danced in their cages all around the floor. They had nothing on this woman right here.

I gently moved her off me then walked to the front door. Just as I got there, there was an audible knock. I opened it, took the bag of groceries one of my men had picked up, and then shut the door again.

Carmen appeared behind me, her shirt pulled down and her tits hidden. "How did you know they were there?"

I set the bag on the counter and pulled everything out. "I just know these things. So, are you hungry?"

She stood beside me and watched me take out the chicken and vegetables, along with a bag of cauliflower rice. "I'm always hungry."

"Really? Because I rarely see you eat."

"Because you make me nervous," she blurted, being honest as always.

I hid the smile that wanted to creep into my mouth, enjoying the fact that I made her tiptoe around me. "Then don't be nervous."

"That's a little difficult when you subtly threaten me all the time."

I folded the bag then turned to her, my veins flooding with testosterone and desire. "Obey me, and you have nothing to worry about."

Her eyes flashed with their usual look of rage. "We both know I'm not good at obeying."

I was hypnotized by her beauty, by those intelligent eyes and sassy persona. She was nothing like the other women I brought home. She had a brain, an attitude, and a fearlessness that made her borderline insane. Every time she defied me, I wanted her more. Every time she stood up to me, I respected her. Every move she made only made my obsession grow, made me hold on to her tighter with no intention of letting her go. "I'm aware."

I turned away and got to work on dinner, letting my subtle aggression fill the air between us. This woman was unconquerable, a woman who wouldn't submit to a man unless he'd earned it. I was up to the challenge. In fact, I was drawn to it. Her constant rejection only made me want her more. There was never a woman I couldn't have—until now. With someone else, they'd be whispering I love you in bed by now. But this woman was too smart for that.

She spotted the other small bag I'd left on the ground in the entryway. "What about this?"

"Leave it." I pulled out all my tools and put the pans on the stove. "I'll show that to you later."

It was one of the rare times she listened to me. She left the bag there and then came to my side. "Can I help?"

"Yes." I pulled her in front of me and gripped her waist with my hands. "Start cutting." My mouth found her neck, and I kissed her as she grabbed the large knife sitting on the cutting board.

She held the handle and turned her head a little, allowing more kisses down her neck. "You trust me with this knife?" She sliced the stalk of asparagus and breathed quietly as she felt me kiss her everywhere.

My fingers moved under her sweater, and I felt the soft skin of her body, touching her piercing before I moved farther up her ribs. "Beautiful, if you stabbed me, I would only want you more. So, go ahead."

9

CARMEN

Bosco wasn't the right man for me. Territorial, aggressive, and threatening, he was the kind of man that could ruin my life. He seemed tame compared to other criminals in the world, but there were always hints of his darker side. If I really wanted to leave, I didn't know if he would let me go.

I was already in so deep.

But all that logic flew out the window once we were in bed together. I didn't think about anything else other than the sexy man on top of me, his chiseled physique and sexy muscles covered in sweat. He was the best lover I'd ever had. There was no comparison to the other men who had been in my bed. Even the best one was laughable compared to Bosco Roth.

I was on my back again, my stomach full with the delicious dinner he'd cooked for me. My thighs hugged his narrow hips, and my ankles were locked together around his waist. With every thrust he made, my tits rose toward my chin before they bounced back again. Without the condom between us, I could feel every groove of his thick cock, even feel the pulsing vein that throbbed as he enjoyed me.

Most of the time, it seemed like a man couldn't keep himself together long enough to bring me to orgasm. They finished the race quickly, some embarrassed and others too satisfied to care.

With Bosco, that was never a problem.

It was all about me.

He still hadn't taken me in any other position; it was always on my back with my tits in his face. His eyes were on me the entire time, watching every expression I made as he fucked me hard one minute, then softly the next.

Why did the best sex of my life have to be with the cruelest man of my life?

I'd already come once, a powerful orgasm that made my thighs nearly bruise his hips. His cock hardened noticeably inside me, but he didn't blow his load. He kept going, his dark gaze on me, burning with arousal.

"This pussy." He breathed in my face, all the muscles of his body contracting as he thrust inside me, his tight ass growing thicker with the movement. "Fuck...this pussy." He sheathed himself to his balls, his length coated in my white cream. He kept driving himself deep inside me, hitting an invisible button that made my body shiver with pleasure.

I gripped his shoulders as I let him drive me deep

into the mattress. This man's desire for me was the biggest turn-on. He could never get enough of me, always taking me aggressively without caring if I did anything in return. All he wanted was to get his huge cock inside me, to give me his come even though he could have any other woman he wanted.

But for right now, he just wanted me.

He was all man, from the muscles in his shoulders to his defined calves. Even his large feet were sexy, covered with cords just like in his forearms. He had rugged hands and chiseled forearms, every inch of his skin vibrating with masculinity.

No other man had made me feel more like a woman.

In the unbridled heat of passion, it seemed like we were something much deeper than what we really were. It seemed like I was the only woman in the world who mattered. And it seemed like he was the man I'd been searching for my whole life.

But once the sex was over, reality would set in once more.

And I would hate him and fear him all over again.

I dragged my nails down his back as I hit my trigger. "Fuck...Bosco." I clung to him harder, taking his big dick in the perfect spot. I'd never felt this full with another man, this slick. It felt so much better without the condom separating us, and the idea of taking his come only turned me on more. "Come inside me... I want all of it. I want to feel your come when I come." I'd never let a man come inside me before, and now I was addicted to it. I loved seeing it drip into my panties, seeing it slide down my thighs when I stood up because it was so heavy.

"Yes, Beautiful." He pressed his face to mine as he thrust into me hard. Outside of sex, he was always the one in charge of calling the shots, but when our naked bodies moved together, he let me make my demands. He got off on pleasing me, like my pleasure was his threshold to a great climax.

His entire body tensed right before he came, his large arms becoming thicker, and the sweat pouring down the back of his neck. With a few more pumps, he released, his heavy come filling my wet cunt. "Take all of it." He shoved himself balls deep and released.

I cried out in his face, having an orgasm even more powerful than the last. My nails nearly cut his skin as they dragged all the way down to his ass. I was so hot, so sweaty, and so out of breath, but I didn't care. "Bosco...I love it when you fuck me." I locked my eyes on to his, seeing the same arousal in his eyes.

He finished with a groan. "I know." He kissed the corner of my mouth before he smothered me with his embrace. He gave me his mouth and his tongue, taking my mouth aggressively like he hadn't just had all of me for the past thirty minutes.

When his cock had softened, he slowly pulled out of me, leaving his seed behind. He rolled over to the spot beside me and lay there, his hand behind his head and his chest shiny with sweat. The glow from the streetlight hit his body, outlining the chiseled grooves of his stomach.

I lay as I was, his come inside me. I pulled my knees to my chest, feeling the heaviness at a deeper angle.

He turned his head toward me and watched me. "You really love my come."

I was still high from coming twice that night, so I didn't think twice before the words came out of my mouth. "Yes." I'd never let a man fuck me without a condom because I'd never been in a monogamous relationship. They were all flings that burned out, not that they ever burned brightly in the first place. I wasn't in a hurry to settle down and pop out some kids, but I was starting to believe it was unlikely I would ever find Mr. Right. The closest I'd gotten was Bosco—and he was completely wrong for me.

"There's plenty more where that came from." He rested his hand against his stomach and closed his eyes, his hard jaw softening now that he was relaxed. He must have shaved that morning because his jaw was free of stubble. Completely smooth, it showed the masculine lines of his face, his perfect features that defined what masculinity should look like.

He suddenly stirred from sleep and grabbed his clothes off the floor. He fished out his phone and set it on the nightstand, like he was expecting a call. He pressed a button on the side of his watch, making a black screen appear over the surface. It was a high-tech gadget I'd never seen.

"What's that?" I whispered.

He faced the ceiling again, closing his eyes. "My team can communicate with me if something comes up."

"So they'll be stationed around my apartment until morning?"

"Not exactly. They'll be dispersed within a three-mile radius, blending in with the surroundings so it's not so obvious they're there. They keep a lookout and notify me of any unusual activity."

"Are these the same men in the lobby of your building."

"No."

He had two dozen men stationed there the entire time, along with a separate crew to escort him everywhere? That was a total of fifty men. I couldn't wrap my mind around that. Conway was a little famous, and he didn't even have that. "Is there something you're afraid of?"

"No." He said it without hesitation. "Men try to approach me all the time, beg me for access to the casino, ask for extensions on their membership dues, bullshit like that. Keeps the beggars away. And if anyone even considers fucking with me, they won't bother when they understand what they're up against. They say just having an alarm system on your home is enough to stop a burglary—same thing."

"So you don't just let anyone in?" Now I found myself more interested in his life. Perhaps I wasn't as afraid to ask questions now that I knew the important stuff. I'd thought if I avoided the truth, it would make it easier. But not knowing just made me more uncomfortable.

"No." He turned his head toward me, his blue eyes serious.

"What are the requirements?"

"A million-dollar annual membership. Criminal background. That's about it."

"Those are pretty big requirements. Why do they have to be a criminal?"

"Because we don't want average men sniffing around. Criminals aren't rats. We won't sell each other out. Regular men don't have balls like we do. You say you want a good man to settle down with and start a family." He shook his head. "Good men are overrated. They're pussies because they aren't brave or strong enough to stand up to anyone and seize greater opportunities. They're lame and boring. Trust me, that's not what you want."

"You don't know me well enough to make that statement."

He didn't blink as he stared me down. "I know everything about you."

"Not possible."

He sat up, propping up his body on his elbow. "I know you're a tough woman who needs a tough man. I know you're drop-dead gorgeous but can't find a man who can handle you. I know you're smart, sassy, and fearless. You need a man who can complement you in every way—but you haven't found him. You can walk into any room and have any man you want—but there are no men good enough for you. If that weren't true, you'd be married. Your problem is you've been looking in the wrong place. Men who follow the rules and live a quiet life are boring. You aren't boring, sweetheart." He lay down again, his heavy frame tilting the mattress slightly in his direction.

"I told you not to call me that." He hadn't done it in a few weeks, but the name had slipped through again.

"Why does it bother you so much?" He turned on his side and faced me, his powerful body rippling with his movements. The sheet clung around his waist, hiding his muscled thighs and long length from view.

"I already said you need to earn the right to call me that—and you never will."

"You know I'm always up for a challenge." He gave me that handsome lopsided grin. "An old boyfriend called you that? Is that why it bothers you?"

"I already told you I've never had a boyfriend."

"I know, but sometimes you act like you've had your heart broken."

"Never." I'd never been in love. The only time I'd experienced real passion was with a man so wrong for me I judged myself for lying beside him at that very moment.

"Then who's earned the right to call you that?" His hand moved to my belly under the sheet, and he gently rubbed me, the same way Griffin rubbed Vanessa's pregnant stomach.

"My father." He'd been calling me that since the day I was born. Carter didn't get a special nickname, but I did. My father hardly used my first name because the nickname was second nature to him. He was overly protective, and he loved me so much that he couldn't think straight most of the time. When he saw Griffin get too close to me, he went ballistic.

It was the first time I'd seen Bosco's eyes soften. He covered up the reaction quickly, like it never happened in the first place. "Alright. That's fair." He scooted closer to me until he was snuggled into my side. He wrapped his powerful arms around me and kept me warm, his thick muscles acting as individual heaters. He pulled my leg over his hip and brought us close together, his face burrowing into my neck.

I'd never been this intertwined with anyone, my legs and arms all over his hard body, but somehow, it was the most comfortable position I'd ever been in. My arm hooked around his neck, and my face rested against his cheek. With his powerful man tangled around me, there was nothing that could ever hurt me. A group of thugs couldn't take me, not when he was there to chase off all the hunters who wanted to take me. He had twenty-four men on the streets surrounding my apartment, making sure no one that didn't belong there could bother either of us. Maybe Bosco was a dangerous man, but having him in my bed made me feel safer than I'd ever been in my life.

It made no sense—but that didn't make it untrue.

A FEW DAYS HAD COME AND GONE, BUT I DIDN'T HEAR from Bosco. He'd crashed at my apartment for the weekend, cooking in the kitchen then fucking me in the bedroom. We didn't talk much, spending most of our time naked and sweaty.

I was at the shop when my brother called me.

"What do you want?" I asked, answering the phone like a bratty sister.

"Hello to you too," he said sarcastically. "I was hoping you could do me a favor."

"Sure. But it's gonna cost you," I teased.

"Mia and I went to Milan for the day so she could pick up her dress. We dropped off Luca at school in the morning and thought we would be back in time to pick him up at the end of the day, but our plane was delayed—"

"Of course, I'll pick him up." I rolled my eyes. "His school is right down the street. I'll take him to get something to eat, and then we'll hang out at my place." Luca had become my nephew, a sweet little boy who was curious about everything. He'd come into my life unexpectedly, but now that he was there, it was hard to imagine life without him.

"Thanks so much, Carmen. We'll see you in a few hours."

I locked up the shop then walked down the street to Luca's school. He attended the best private school in the city, something Carter had set up. I moved through the gates, and when the bell rang, Luca came out with his dinosaur backpack. He was initially confused when he didn't see his mom, but when he saw me, he ran into my arms. "Aunt Carmen!"

I kneeled down and opened my arms, sweeping him into a big hug. "Hey, Luca. Do you mind if I pick you up today?"

"No! Where's my mom, though?" He wore a red t-shirt with stripes and jeans that were a little baggy for his long legs.

"She and Carter had an errand to run. They'll pick you up in a few hours."

"Okay." I grabbed his hand, and we started to walk down the sidewalk. "You want to get some lunch?"

"Yeah," Luca said. "Ice cream."

I raised my eyebrow as I looked down at him. "We both know you don't get ice cream for lunch. But nice try."

He laughed, slightly embarrassed that I'd figured out he was trying to trick me.

We went to a café, and he got a sandwich and an applesauce. Then we walked home, the afternoon air already cold. The sun set early now that it was winter, so it was already dark halfway home.

That was when I noticed a strange man walking toward me, dressed in all black and looking suspicious. His eyes were on me, noticing Luca beside me. I'd heard horror stories about people snatching kids, and I'd rather die than let that happen. I held his gaze and kept Luca close beside me, ready to rip both of the man's eyes out if he tried something. I should have taken a cab, but enjoying Luca's company distracted me from what was important.

Before the guy even reached me, another man emerged and stopped in front of him. Dressed in jeans and a black sweater, he was muscular with short hair. He reminded me of one of Bosco's men, who all possessed the same look. He stared the man down but didn't make a scene. His look seemed to be enough because the man turned around went back the way he came.

As if nothing had happened, the man walked away and leaned against the wall, watching me while trying to be discreet about it.

I crossed the street, my heart still beating fast. Something told me that was one of Bosco's men, and he had a security team following me around everywhere I went. Initially, I was pissed that he'd breached my privacy like that.

But then I felt nothing but gratitude.

Maybe that man wasn't going to do anything at all. Maybe I was just being paranoid.

Or maybe he was going to rob me at gunpoint and scar Luca forever.

Or even worse, he was gonna take Luca away from me.

Now I would never have to find out.

WE SAT AT THE KITCHEN TABLE TOGETHER WHILE LUCA completed his homework. He snacked on a plate of sliced apples while he worked on his sheets. Sometimes he asked me for help, and I was relieved I was able to help him. Math had always been my strongest subject, but I would have been embarrassed if I'd forgotten my basic skills.

A knock sounded on the door. "That must be your mom." I checked the peephole first before I let them inside. "Hey, guys. How's it going?"

Mia hugged me and kissed me on the cheek. "So great. We went to pick up my wedding dress. Conway had a special designer make it for me."

"Wow, that was nice. I bet it's beautiful."

Mia went to Luca at the kitchen table and kissed him on the head. "Hey, sweetheart. Did you have a fun day?"

Carter came inside next, nearly a foot taller than me. Looking at him made me realize he and Bosco were the same height. Thinking about the dangerous man I was sleeping with suddenly made me feel guilty since Carter would never approve. "Did you see the dress?"

"No," he said quickly. "I just took her down there. We had lunch, spent some time together."

It was hard to believe my manwhore brother was getting married. He'd never had a girlfriend in his life, and then he met Mia under the worst circumstances, and that changed his life forever.

"How was Luca?"

"Great, as usual. We had lunch, and he's been working on his homework ever since."

"He's a good kid," Carter said proudly.

"Very sweet."

Carter walked to him and kissed him on the head. "How's my little man?"

"Great!" He picked up his math homework. "Aunt Carmen helped me finish it."

"That's awesome." Carter helped him pack his stuff into his backpack. "Let's get going. Mom's gotta get dinner on the table."

"Alright." Luca put on his backpack then walked up to me. "Thanks for picking me up, Aunt Carmen."

My heart melted into a puddle for this little boy. He was so sweet, had a heart of gold. I'd always wanted a family of my own, but being around Luca just made me realize how much I needed it. I kneeled down and hugged him tightly, squeezing him against my chest and smelling his hair. My ovaries were practically screaming because I wanted to be a mother even more than I had before. "You're welcome, Luca." I finally released him and stood up.

Mia put her hand on his shoulder and guided him into the hallway.

Carter lingered behind for a second. "Thanks for picking him up."

"I didn't mind at all," I said with a sigh.

Carter stared at me for a moment, his eyes turning

serious. We'd never been very close, not the way I was with Vanessa, but we got along well enough. He'd always been protective of me, showing me he loved me rather than ever saying it. "It'll happen for you someday, Carmen."

"What?" I asked.

"A family." He touched my shoulder gently before he pulled away. "Just be patient. The right guy is out there looking for you."

That mythical man was nowhere to be found. And the man I was currently sleeping with certainly wasn't the one. "I hope you're right."

I STILL HADN'T HEARD FROM BOSCO, WHICH WAS UNUSUAL since we talked every few days. Now four days had passed without a word from him.

I wondered if he'd gotten bored with me.

I decided to call him as I sat on the couch, wool socks on my feet and wearing a baggy sweater.

He answered almost immediately. "Beautiful." It was quiet in the background, making me think he was home.

"Bosco."

He chuckled slightly. "It doesn't matter what context it is, hearing you say my name is the sexiest thing I've ever heard."

Maybe he wasn't bored with me, after all. I wondered why he hadn't called, but I refused to ask. That would make me seem clingy, and I didn't want to be clingy with him. He was the worst man in the world to feel attached to. Not only would he break my heart, but he would destroy me. "Are your men following me around?" I asked the question that was on my mind, pretending that was the only reason I was calling. I was too proud to invite him over, to tell him I missed him.

He was quiet for a while, drawing out the silence before he finally gave his answer. "Yes."

I knew he would be honest, so I didn't expect any other answer. There was no way that man had interfered by coincidence. There had been no one on the sidewalk just a second before, and then out of nowhere, that man appeared.

"I won't apologize for it. I won't justify it. If it pisses you off, I don't give a damn. I just want to be upfront about that to save you some time."

I didn't expect anything else. "How long have you had your men following me?"

"Since the beginning."

"Why?"

"To keep your safe, obviously. I have ten men tailing you at all times."

"Ten?" I asked incredulously.

"Yes," he said unapologetically. "Maybe I'll make it twenty after what happened the other day."

So he did know about it. "Who was he?"

"You don't want to know."

He was right, I didn't.

"But I took care of it personally. Don't think about him again."

"What does that mean?" I asked, unsure if I wanted the answer.

"I stabbed him to death and left him in a dumpster."

I closed my eyes, cringing at the gruesome image in my head.

"And don't feel bad about it—trust me."

The man probably deserved it. I didn't want to know what his crimes were. But if he'd really wanted to take Luca away from me, he deserved the gruesome death he'd experienced. "I'm starting to wonder if Florence is the most dangerous place on earth."

"No, not even close. But there are bad men everywhere. You're fucking one of them."

He had me there.

"Are you angry with me?" he asked, his voice suddenly softer.

"No." If that intervention saved Luca, I should only feel grateful. That little boy was pure and innocent. If anything ever happened to him, I would lose my shit and go ballistic. I would stab a man twenty times before leaving him in a dumpster.

"You're always safe with me, Beautiful—even when I'm not there."

Even as I sat in my apartment, a sense of relief washed over me. It cleansed my heart and my blood, made me feel at peace with the world. Even if there were a murderer lingering outside my apartment, he would never get to me. When I had a man like Bosco in my life, I never had to feel scared again.

"As I've told you, you can walk the streets naked if you want—nothing will happen to you."

I believed it.

"Walk home in the dark. Do whatever the fuck you want. You're my woman—and you're untouchable." Like the conversation was over, he hung up on me. He didn't ask to see me or try to come over. He was possessive with me but then cold. It didn't make any sense.

I almost called him back—but my pride wouldn't allow it.

———

"WHO THE HELL IS THAT?" I WHISPERED TO VANESSA AS we stood in front of the painting while nodding to her desk.

A large man sat there, dressed in a collared shirt and dark jeans. He didn't look like the kind of man that belonged in a gallery, not with those cold looks and extremely short hair. He reminded me of Griffin—grim and angry.

Vanessa didn't follow my gaze. "My new assistant."

I gave her an incredulous look, not buying that story one bit.

She rolled her eyes and walked out with me as we headed to lunch. "Griffin doesn't like me being here alone. He knows he needs to be at the winery, so he had me hire an assistant...but he doesn't actually help me."

"He just protects you."

"Yep." She walked beside me and turned into the café where we were about to eat. "He's retired and has a family of his own. He was looking for easy work that would get him home by five every day. So Griffin asked him to watch me during business hours."

"That's sweet."

"I tried to fight Griffin off in the beginning, but it wasn't working. He said it was hard enough to leave me alone just as his wife, but now that I'm having his baby... he said he couldn't stand the idea." We both ordered then took a seat by the window.

"Understandable."

"I wanted to keep fighting, but I knew it was an argument I would never win, so I just caved. That's what marriage is all about—deciding the right time to cave."

"He's just trying to protect you. I can't say that I blame him."

"I can't either," she said with a sigh. "His heart is in the right place, so it's fine." She rubbed her stomach gently as it protruded through her sweater. "The baby has been kicking a lot lately. Griffin is fascinated by it."

"Wow, that's so great." Seeing Vanessa married and pregnant gave me a hint of jealousy. I'd never been that way before, but seeing Luca the other day made me realize how much I wanted a family. Listening to how Griffin protected her made me realize I wanted that too.

Bosco fulfilled the second part, but he could never fulfill the first.

"Do you think it's a boy or a girl?" I asked.

"Hmm...it's hard to tell." She removed her hand from her stomach and sipped her water. "But I think it's a boy. He just kicks so much, even though it's not too hard yet, like he needs to take up as much space as possible. He's aggressive and bossy, making me throw up in the morning sometimes. So, it's probably a boy." She laughed. "Reminds me of Griffin."

I chuckled. "You're probably right."

"So, what's up with Mr. Panty Soaker?" she asked. "Are you still hooking up with him?" Unlike before, Vanessa ate her food quickly, her appetite forcing her to dig into her meal like she hadn't eaten in days. She'd never had an appetite before, but now everything was different.

"Yeah...I'm still seeing him." As far as Vanessa knew, this secret guy was just some random man who didn't matter. In reality, I was in pretty deep with a dangerous man that I should stay away from. It was getting difficult to hide it—especially from her. I wasn't sure what I was doing anymore, and that scared me.

"Really?" she asked. "So, it's been a few weeks, then?"

"Yeah, about three."

"That's a pretty long time for just sleeping together..." She gave me a look full of accusation, her opinion written directly across her face. "Sounds like it's a little more serious. Do you actually like this guy?"

"Yes. And no."

"What do you like about him?"

I considered my answer for a long time before I gave it. "I like that he's strong. He's the protective type...like Griffin." Bosco had saved me twice now, once when he wasn't even there. He had the entire city under his control, giving me the power to walk freely without fear of harassment. He gave me something no one else ever could, not even my father.

"That was never important to me either, but after what happened with Knuckles, Griffin became exactly what I was looking for. It's nice to know you always have him to protect you, even if you never need it. I guess it's something all women are looking for...not realizing it until they find it. Men won't even look at me when Griffin is around. He's like the biggest shark in the ocean, and all the other men are fish."

That was the same description I would give to Bosco.

"What else?" she asked.

"He's has a sweet side..."

"Like roses and chocolates?" she asked.

I almost laughed because that was something Bosco would never do. "He speaks highly of his mother, who passed away a few years ago from cancer. She was a single mother who raised him and his brother, and he always has this respect in his voice...like he was so proud of her. He took care of her for the last ten years of her life. Since I'm so close to my family, I liked hearing that he is close to his."

"That is sweet," she said. "I like him already."

She shouldn't draw a conclusion just yet. "A lot of men I meet are a bit turned off by my headstrong attitude. They're either intimidated or annoyed by it."

"I know how that is," she said with a chuckle.

"But it doesn't bother him at all. In fact, I think it's the reason he likes me so much."

She nodded. "Griffin told me only a truly powerful man can handle a powerful woman. Only a man so secure in who he is would be unaffected by her. So if he actually likes those qualities about you, that means he's one hell of a man. At least in my experience…"

"So…those are all the things I like about him. Not to mention, the sex is incredible." Now that it'd been almost a week since he'd been between my legs, I was starting to get grouchy. I wondered what he was doing at night and if he was thinking about me. Was he so busy he didn't have time for me? Or was he with someone else? That didn't seem likely because he would be transparent about it.

"It sounds like he's the perfect man. So, what's the problem? Why don't you make it into something more?" Vanessa took a bite of her sandwich and quickly swallowed it down. "It sounds like your dad would like him, based on everything you just told me."

This time, I couldn't stop myself from laughing.

"What?" she asked, visibly confused. "Unless there's something you aren't telling me…"

I knew Vanessa would keep my secret if I asked her

to. Regardless of her relationship with her husband, she would keep my secret safe. Her loyalty to him had nothing to do with her loyalty to me. "There's a lot I haven't told you. But I need you to understand that this has to stay between us. You can't even tell Griffin."

She wiped her mouth with a napkin then sighed. "Oh shit. This is bad, isn't it?"

I nodded. "Really bad. Can you keep a secret?"

She rolled her eyes. "Girl, you know I can. That's not what I'm worried about. Who is this guy you're involved with?"

"You remember my incident in the alleyway?"

"Unfortunately," she said coldly. "Instead of letting those guys get away, Bosco should have—" Like a light-bulb went off in her head, she darted her gaze to me, her eyes expanded to the size of baseballs. "Oh. My. God. It's Bosco, isn't it?"

I nodded, feeling the guilt rise in my stomach.

"Oh shit." She threw her napkin down. "Griffin has nothing but bad things to say about that guy."

"I'm aware."

"Then what the hell are you doing?" she demanded. "Griffin made it sound like he's a psycho dictator. He controls the entire city. The guy is untouchable. He's basically the king of this entire area. Not only does he control the police, the government, and the cash, but he also controls all the murderers, thieves, and rapists. He's like...the head honcho."

"Yeah..." That described him pretty well.

"Then what are you doing, Carmen?"

I sighed and tucked my hair behind my ear. "I have no idea. It started off slow and then escalated into this... I'm not sure what to do."

"How did this happen? He saved you, and then you took him home?"

"Not quite," I said. "After he saved me, he said he wanted something in return."

"Ahh...here we go." She shook her head, as if this didn't surprise her at all. "And he asked you to fuck him to show your gratitude. Been there...done that."

"He asked for a kiss, actually. But it turned into a dry hump that made me come in the alleyway." I wouldn't share this embarrassing information with anyone else but her, knowing she wouldn't judge me for it. "Then I went home, alone, and assumed I would never see him again. But then he showed up at my work, crashed a date I had, and it just kept getting worse. So we started hooking up, and that's all it was supposed to be...meaningless sex. But then he said he wanted a chance to be something more...and here I am now. He has men tail me everywhere I go to keep me safe, he says I belong to him now, and before I knew what happened, I was basically in a monogamous relationship with this guy." I was talking a million miles a minute, so I finally paused and caught my breath.

Vanessa stared at me, speechless. "Jesus."

"Yeah..."

"Does he hurt you?"

"No," I blurted. "Not at all. He's protective...even kind. He's just a little intense. Said he doesn't want to share me with anyone, and he doesn't want to be with anyone else either. So he pretty much decided that we're exclusive."

"And what does that mean?" she asked. "Are you serious, then? Is this actually something?"

"No. I told him I would never want any kind of future with him."

"Good."

"It's just a monogamous fling...because he doesn't want to wear a condom."

"Girl, did you—"

"He gave me his papers. He's clean."

"Good...maybe he's somewhat of a gentleman, after all."

I scoffed, thinking that was a bit of a stretch. "He told me Griffin threatened him to stay away from me."

"Why didn't you tell Griffin when this started?"

"Because of everything you just said," I snapped. "This guy has twenty-four men guarding him at any given time. He has another team at the building he owns too. This guy throws lawbreakers into a ring and makes them fight to the death. You think I'm getting Griffin involved in that? When you guys are having a baby? Hell no, I'm keeping this a secret from everyone —except you."

Vanessa's eyes softened. "I appreciate that, Carmen, but we're family. You're like a sister to me. Whatever happens to one of us, happens to all of us. We're in this together. And if you need to get out of this relationship, we'll make it happen."

"That's the thing…" I broke eye contact because I couldn't look at her as I spoke. "I'm not sure if I want out of this relationship…" I would never find a man who could please me like Bosco. I would never find a man who could protect me the way he could. "And even if I did, I'm not sure if I have a choice. He's made subtle threats here and there…that he'll never let me go."

"Shit," she whispered. "From what I've learned, you have to stand your ground."

I nodded. "He told me the same thing."

"Do you see a future with this guy?" she asked, watching me closely.

I still didn't like Bosco for what he did for a living. I was still afraid of him, afraid of the power that was constantly at his fingertips. Getting involved with a man like that sounded dangerous. His enemies would be my enemies. "I've always pictured a house in Tuscany with four kids. I would sell the shop and be a full-time mom. My husband…he doesn't really have a face, but he's there. I don't know anything about him, but he's kind and strong. That's the future I want, and I definitely can't picture Bosco fitting into that image."

"If he doesn't fit in that vision, then he's probably not the right guy. But based on my experience with Griffin, I didn't think that future was possible with him either. But slowly, he started to be part of that picture. Now he's the greatest husband I ever could have asked for...because he grew into the man I wanted him to be."

"I don't think Bosco would change for anyone..."

"Then maybe you should get out of this relationship...if you still can."

The idea of finding Mr. Right didn't sound appealing since he didn't seem to exist. I didn't want to go back to mediocre sex either, not when Bosco gave me mind-blowing sex every single time. He was so selfless in bed, aroused by my pleasure more than his own. And I loved feeling safe, knowing that nothing would ever happen to me as long as I was the woman in his bed. But if I got any deeper into this relationship, then I might never be able to crawl out. He might become more obsessed with me.

And he might not let me go. "Yeah, you're right..."

ANOTHER TWO DAYS PASSED, AND HE DIDN'T CALL ME.

It'd been a week now.

None of this was making sense. Maybe he didn't want me anymore. Maybe he didn't care anymore. That would make my escape much easier, but it also pained me at the same time.

That he was bored of me so quickly.

I was lying in bed alone, the wool socks on my feet to keep me warm. It was late, but I couldn't sleep, the area between my legs throbbing because Bosco hadn't been there in so long. If he wasn't sleeping with anyone else, then he must be going crazy too.

The thought of him sleeping with someone else pissed me off, not because I was jealous, but because he wasn't man enough to tell me about it. Was he just going to ignore me forever and assume I would disappear? Did that mean his men weren't guarding me anymore? Our last conversation made it sound like we were still together, but his silence said otherwise.

My emotion dominated my logic, and I picked up the phone and called him.

He answered almost instantly. "Beautiful."

I stared at the ceiling, annoyed by the confident sound of his masculine voice. "Don't call me that."

He turned silent.

I stayed silent too, unsure what to say because I was angry at him.

He didn't speak, letting the silence continue indefinitely. He didn't ask what was wrong, like he knew exactly what the problem was.

"Are you sleeping with someone else?" I asked bluntly, knowing he would tell me the truth.

A smile was audible in his voice. "No."

"You aren't?" I asked incredulously, expecting a different answer.

"No." That was all he gave me, but that single-word answer was still full of his amusement.

Now I really had no idea what was going on. I hadn't seen him for an entire week. He didn't give me any explanation, and it seemed like I would never get one unless I asked for it. Maybe he was doing that on purpose.

"You're angry I haven't called."

I refused to acknowledge the assumption, especially since he hit the nail right on the head.

"You miss me."

I definitely wouldn't admit that.

"I'm all yours." His deep voice was elementally soothing, making me feel aroused and safe at the same time. "I've been yours. I've slept alone in this bed every single night. All you have to do is tell me that you need me, that you miss me, and I'll be there in ten minutes."

This was all a game to him—and I was losing.

"Tell me that you need me."

I refused.

"Beautiful, one of the reasons I adore you is your bluntness. You're the kind of woman that asks for what she wants, isn't afraid to tell a man how to fuck her. You aren't timid and shy. You're strong and unapologetic. If you want me—tell me."

Humiliation flooded my end of the line. He had me cornered. That was exactly how I was, and the reason I wasn't doing it now was because I was ashamed of my emotions, ashamed that my feelings had grown. I'd never chased him before, but now I was the one calling him. He'd turned the tables on our relationship—making me pursue him instead.

"Tell me what you want." His quiet breathing floated over the line. I pictured him lying in bed, sleeping in his black boxers with his enormous bulge in the front. I imagined the sleepy look on his face, the subtle stubble along his jaw. I imagined those beautiful blue eyes, the ones that looked into me so deeply.

"I hate you."

"I know you do, Beautiful. But you need me more than you hate me. I could be between your legs right now, pleasuring you the way a real man should. You could be coming around my dick and asking for another round because I'm not a boy who can't control his load. I could be keeping your sheets warm, making you abandon those thick wool socks you only wear when I'm not there. I could be chasing away your demons, making you sleep soundly knowing a man can never get past me to you. All of this could happen...but you have to ask for it."

I felt like a person addicted to drugs. I took a few hits thinking I could handle a taste. But before I knew it, I was blindly hooked on the sensation, needing it beyond reason. Now I was buying more, even though I was utterly ashamed for needing it so much.

His tone turned more aggressive. "Say it."

The command in his voice made my thighs press together. I missed him so much that I couldn't think logically. I was fine before he came along, indifferent to him completely. But now, I was the one crawling to him—on my hands and knees. "I want you..." A wave of self-loathing washed over me. I despised myself for giving in, but I was also relieved I was finally getting what I wanted

—regardless of the price I'd just paid. I'd traded my dignity and self-respect in exchange for this man, a man I didn't even like.

Click.

MY DOOR OPENED TEN MINUTES LATER, THE LOCKS DOING nothing to keep him out.

I stayed in bed, knowing he would figure out exactly where I was. I listened to his footsteps as they pounded down the hallway, his heavy frame causing the sounds to echo off the walls. I'd already taken my clothes off because I didn't want to waste any time getting undressed.

He came through the door, pulling his shirt off in the process. His belt clanked in the darkness as he loosened it and got his jeans off. He stood at the foot of my bed, looking down at me with victory in his eyes. His chin was clean from shaving recently, and his hair was styled like he hadn't been sleeping at all—but waiting for my phone call.

Every piece of clothing hit the floor until he stood with his enormous erection, thick and throbbing. He gave me a more intense look than I'd ever seen, like he hated me for waiting an entire week to finally make the call.

Over six feet of pure beauty, he towered over my bed with the body of a Greek god. From strong shoulders to thick arms, he had the perfect physique of a ruler. With thick thighs that bulged with muscle to abs that had more strength than both of my arms to put together, he was dangerously sexy.

My lungs forgot to breathe.

His knees hit the bed, making the mattress dip, and he maneuvered on top of me, kicking away the sheets and opening my legs so he could get to get my soaking cunt. He kept up that aggressive stare, like he wanted to backhand me for making him wait this long to fuck me.

He positioned me underneath him, tilting my hips perfectly and pressing his arms into the mattress on either side of my tits. He stared down at me with a slight scowl on his face. "Tell me you missed me." He was going to drag this out even more, demoralize me for making that phone call. He wanted to fill me with shame, to remind me that he had all the power in this relationship —even the power I'd once had.

My hands gripped his arms, and I sighed in relief at his warmth. Touching him brought me a sense of joy that I couldn't understand. I needed him even more than I'd realized, more than my brain would allow me to understand.

He pressed the head of his cock inside me, stretching me slightly. "Say it."

My hand moved into the back of his hair, and I pulled his face to mine to kiss him. "I missed you..." The weight was lifted off my shoulders as I made my confession. I wanted him so badly, to the exclusion of all less.

Until I got my next fix, I would say anything he wanted me to say. I needed this intense passion more than I needed air or food. I needed this man buried deep inside me, to please me since it'd been so long since he'd last fulfilled my needs.

"Tell me you need me." He kept making his commands, knowing I would obey.

"I need you..." I grabbed his hip and slowly pulled him inside me.

He stopped himself, not entering me any farther. He fisted my hair and forced my gaze on his. "Say it again."

"I need you, Bosco." I held his gaze, my lips parted and desperate for his kiss.

"Tell me you don't want me to sleep with anyone else. Tell me it would drive you crazy."

"I don't want you to sleep with anyone else..." Just the thought pissed me off. When he didn't call, I'd assumed he'd found someone else, and it made me feel so low. "I want you to only sleep with me."

He sank a little deeper, rewarding me for my obedience. "You were angry I didn't call."

"Yes...I was."

He moved in deeper, stretching me so good. "Tell me when you want me. Call me when you need me. Use me when you want to be used. Do you understand me?"

"Yes..." I just wanted him to start moving, to make my toes curl with a perfect climax.

"Now beg me to fuck you. Beg."

"You're such a fucking asshole."

He sank deeper, sheathing himself until he was balls deep. He wore that handsome lopsided grin. "I know, Beautiful. But you love fucking this asshole. Now, beg." He didn't move, resting deep inside me as he watched me squirm.

"Please..."

"Louder."

"Please." I dragged my hands down his back and panted against his mouth. "Fuck me, Bosco. Please..."

He pressed a soft kiss to my lips. "Good job." He started to move, thrusting into me deep and hard. The headboard began to tap against the wall immediately because he took me so hard right in the beginning. He ground against me, making my clit catch on fire and my back arch in impossible ways.

I held on to him tightly as he screwed me better than he ever had before, going right for the perfect spot and making me come within a minute flat. I was probably just turned on like crazy, but he pushed me to the finish line with his stellar moves. His fat cock was big enough to make me writhe, to make me shake because it felt so perfect inside me. "God...yes." My head rolled back, and I clawed at him viciously, pulling him closer against me as I widened my legs farther, squeezing his dick so hard with my powerful orgasm.

"So fucking wet."

"I'm always wet for you..."

"I know." He hooked his arms behind my knees and

deepened the angle, preparing to fuck me again and give me another climax.

"Bosco, I want you to make me come two more times..." It'd been an entire week without pleasure, and I was losing my mind. That first climax, while wonderful, wasn't enough to fill my hunger.

He stopped moving, looking down at me with a slight grin on his face. "There's my woman..."

10

BOSCO

WHEN I WOKE up the next morning, Carmen was on top of my chest. As time passed, she snuggled with me more and more. And now she was curled up on me like a cat. The only thing missing was the sound of her purring.

I moved my hand through her hair and pulled it from her face, so I could get a better look at those plump lips and beautiful cheeks. She looked softer than a rose petal when she was asleep, peaceful knowing nothing could get through me to her.

Her alarm sounded a second later, making her jerk slightly at the obnoxious noise.

The serene moment ended.

She reached across the bed to her nightstand and shut off the alarm. "Ugh..." She yawned and ran her fingers through her hair, slowly waking up after the long night we had. We didn't fall asleep until a few hours ago.

She moved back to me, hugging me like a pillow. Her hair brushed against my skin, soft like a feather. She finally directed her eyes on me, and as the memory of last night flooded her mind, her cheeks began to redden noticeably. Then she looked away altogether, ashamed she'd given in so profoundly.

I enjoyed every second of it.

She needed to be reminded that she needed me, that I wasn't just some man she was sleeping with. She could pretend I meant nothing to her, but we both knew that wasn't true anymore. I could feel her rage over the phone, how pissed she'd been that I hadn't called her all week. She wanted to keep pretending to be indifferent to me, but I took that away from her.

Now I'd evened the score.

She moved away from me and rose to her feet. "I've got to get to work."

I couldn't wipe the grin off my face, loving the way she loathed herself from submitting to me so completely. She'd missed me like crazy. I already knew it before she told me, but it was still nice to hear. Maybe I was an asshole—but I was her asshole.

She pulled on a pair of jeans from the floor and then clasped her nude bra around her waist.

I watched her before I got out of bed and pulled on my clothes.

She skipped the makeup, but brushed her teeth and fixed her hair before she left the room and walked to the front of the apartment.

I followed her, watching her heart-shaped ass shake.

She grabbed her purse and pulled it over her shoulder, her phone stuffed into her back pocket. She kept avoiding eye contact, unable to meet me head on.

I grabbed her by the elbow and yanked her toward me, making her face me to look me dead in the eye.

Now she held my gaze without blinking.

"No more games." My arm circled her waist and pulled her deeper into me. I gripped her lower back and let my lips hover above hers. "You look me in the eye when you tell me goodbye. You call me when you want me. You treat me like I'm yours—not some dirty secret. Do you understand me?"

She knew it would be stupid to defy me, not after the way I made her crumble into pieces last night. "Yes..."

I kissed the corner of her mouth. "Tell me I make you feel safe."

Her arms hooked around my neck, and she pressed her forehead against mine. "You make me feel safe." Not only did she repeat the words, but it sounded like she meant them. I didn't need to be between her legs to make her cooperate—because I'd already conquered her.

"Have a good day at work." I kissed her on the mouth before I walked out the door, saying goodbye like a man did to his wife.

I heard her voice trail behind me as I left. "Thanks...you too."

I WAS SITTING IN MY OFFICE WHEN DRAKE KNOCKED AND walked inside. "Sir?"

I was doing the bookkeeping, making sure no one was hacking in to our systems and stealing our cash. The memberships people paid kept the casino going. I took my share every month as a salary for keeping the place going, along with insurance and liability. In addition to that, I gambled myself. All payments were transferred digitally, so there was no cash in the building.

The men would be too tempted to rob me.

"Come in." I quickly logged out of the account, cleared my history, and then shut the laptop. I didn't take chances with anyone—except Ronan. "What's up?" I glanced at the only picture on my desk, a picture of Ronan and me with my mother. It was taken a year before she was diagnosed with cancer. It was Christmas morning—and I'd bought her a car.

Drake approached my desk, visibly tired after his long shift with Carmen. "I eavesdropped on a conversation Carmen had with Vanessa. I'm not sure if this is information you want to know, but I thought I would ask."

I had my men tail her everywhere she went, joining her in restaurants and posing as potential flower shop customers whenever someone remotely shady entered her store. It didn't seem like she aware of it, minus the pedophile who almost tried to touch her nephew. She had no idea how extensively I controlled every inch of this city. But my intention had never been to invade her privacy. I didn't spy on her inside her apartment, and I didn't tap her phone lines or listen to her private conversations. "Is there a problem?"

"There's no problem with her safety. But she talked about you—and told the truth."

I froze on the spot, shocked that she'd told her cousin the truth about me.

"She asked Vanessa not to share the information with Bones."

I wondered if she would keep her promise. "What else was said?"

"Vanessa told Carmen she should stay away from you. They talked about it for a while, and then Carmen said she didn't see a future with you, that she's afraid you won't let her go when she wants to leave...and you aren't right for her." Drake looked awkward telling me this, like he wished he were doing anything else besides discussing my personal life.

I felt the rage circulate in my veins, the fact that Carmen actually considered trying to get rid of me.

"Said she wants a house in Tuscany with her husband and four kids—and her husband will never be you."

I didn't give a shit how she pictured her fairy-tale life. Fairy tales weren't real, and no other man would give her what she really wanted. No other man would be able to handle this woman, provide for her and protect her. She needed to forget about that happily ever after because it would never happen. "That'll be all, Drake."

He took the dismissal and walked out.

I sat in my leather chair, my office not having any windows because it was protected by layers of concrete on every single side. The only way inside was up a long staircase that led to an elevator that could only be accessed with a special card.

I was a bit paranoid.

No one had ever made an attempt on my life, probably because the chance of success was so small. But that didn't mean it wouldn't happen someday. When it did, I would be prepared.

I was prepared for anything.

I considered Carmen's gossip with her cousin and wondered when that conversation had taken place. It must have happened before she called me, pissed off that I'd ignored her all week and desperate to have me again. Maybe she knew I was bad for her, but that wouldn't change how much she needed me.

She wasn't strong enough to leave me.

If she were, she wouldn't have gotten in this deep to begin with.

And if she did find the courage to walk away from me, it would be the greatest mistake she ever made.

Because she would find out what kind of monster I really was.

I REFILLED MY GLASS AS I SAT ON THE COUCH, THE TV ON in the background. I was reading a book, wearing just my fitted black sweatpants without a shirt. It didn't matter that it was freezing cold outside.

I was always warm.

I hadn't called Carmen because I wanted her to make the first move—to remind her how far she was under my thumb.

She texted me, her words popping up on my screen. *I just got home from work.*

I grinned when I saw her name flash across my phone. I had seen her that morning—and put her in her place. I grabbed my phone and wrote back. *How was your day?*

Slow. Didn't make a single sale.

It happens. I didn't invite her over or head to her place. I'd been doing nothing but chasing this woman around. It was her turn to chase me.

She didn't write back for a while, probably hating herself for messaging me at all, treating me like I was some kind of boyfriend.

I definitely wasn't her boyfriend. Boyfriends were for pussies.

I was her man.

She finally messaged me again. *My place or yours?*

I liked her choice of words, keeping her dignity as much as possible. She asked for what she wanted but did it with pride. *One of my men will be at your door in three minutes. He'll bring you to my place. Pack a bag.* I put the phone down and kept reading, enjoying my scotch while I waited for Carmen to be delivered right to my door.

I MET HER DOWNSTAIRS AND TOOK HER UP IN THE ELEVATOR since I was the only one who had access to the code.

She was dressed in tight jeans, boots, and a black jacket. Her hair was styled, and her makeup was fresh, like she'd redone it before coming over.

I took the bag from her hand and placed the strap over my shoulder. I wasn't a gentleman, but I didn't mind doing things for her, making her feel desired and taken care of. It was only a minute to the top of the building, but my hands circled her waist and I kissed her, giving her soft embraces that teased her lips more than satisfied them. My hand moved to her hair, and I felt her melt at my touch, her breathing immediately changing and her muscles tightening.

The doors opened, and I grabbed her hand and guided her into my penthouse.

She looked around the living room again, the same mesmerized look on her face as the last time she was here.

I set her bag on the rug and grabbed the bottle I'd been pouring from. "Would you like one?"

"Sure."

I filled her glass before I sat on the couch. I turned off

the TV and closed the book I'd been reading. Once that was done, I gave her all of my attention, focusing my hard gaze on her, burning her with the intensity of my stare.

She stopped in front of the couch and pulled her jacket off before she tossed it on the ground. Then she removed her shirt and her jeans, stripping down to a sexy ensemble. Her lingerie was a matching set, lacy black panties and a see-through bra. She straddled my hips and sank down into my lap, her shoulders back and her tits in my face. Her hands moved up my bare chest until she gripped my broad shoulders. With her green eyes locked on mine and her hair framing her face, she said the sexiest thing. "I missed you..." She dragged her hands down my chest, her fingertips following the grooves in my abs.

I'd had a lot of women in my lap just like this, but none of them was as beautiful as she. My hands glided up her thighs until I reached her hips. I gave her a gentle squeeze, feeling the delicate lace of her panties. Everything about her was perfect, from the olive color of her skin, to the small muscles of her arms and stomach, to her large bust. "I missed you too, Beautiful." I held her gaze as I said the words, meaning every single syllable. There was nothing sexier than watching this woman want me, than watching her wear her heart on her sleeve. I didn't think it was possible.

I hoped this meant she'd changed her mind about her conversation with Vanessa.

Because I certainly hadn't changed mine.

She sank deeper into me, pressing her tits against my chest as she wrapped her arms around my neck.

My hands glided over her perky ass, my fingers feeling the lace of her panties. "This is the first time in my life I've bedded just one woman. I've been with lovely people, but none of them has had your special charm. Every time I have you, I want more of you. Instead of speeding up and finishing, I want to please you the way you please me." I pressed the backs of my fingers against her cheek and gently caressed her soft skin, dragging my fingers down her neck. "You're perfect. Fucking perfect." I wrapped my fingers around her neck next, feeling her slow and steady pulse under my grip.

She leaned in closer to me and pressed her lips against mine, giving me a soft kiss as her fingers explored my short hair. She breathed into me gently, her lips quivering slightly with desire.

I kept my hand around her neck, loving the way I had complete power over this woman. Her hatred couldn't defeat her desire. Her pussy still dripped for me, her thighs still opened for me. She would never try to leave, not when she settled into my body so easily.

I rested my head back and looked up at her, treasuring the sight of this beautiful woman on top of me. I'd had more women than I could count, meeting them at the casino, the strip clubs, or just on the street. The ones who knew me wanted me for my money and my power. It made them wet instantly. Carmen was different because she wasn't impressed by expensive things. She actually disliked me, but she wanted me so much, she couldn't stay away. That was how I knew this was real—and I didn't want it to end.

"Never?" she whispered, referring to what I'd said a moment ago.

"Never." I tucked her hair behind her ear, revealing more of her beautiful face. "You're the only woman I've screwed without a condom."

Her eyes flashed like that meant something to her. "I'm sure the other girls would have skipped the rubber if you'd asked...because they would have done anything for you."

I didn't want a woman who would do anything for me. I wanted a woman who didn't need me. I wanted Carmen. "Not interested in that. I'm don't like women who give up everything for one guy."

"Interesting," she whispered. "Because it seems like you want me to give up everything—like my freedom."

"Yes. But you fight me every step of the way. I admire that."

"You admire me for fighting you?" she asked. "You don't want a submissive woman who does whatever she's told? It seems like you would—because that's what you're always asking me to do."

"I guess not." I'd never given it much thought. Pussy was pussy. I'd sunk into different ones on a nightly basis. They were all wet, all tight, and all beautiful. But when I set eyes on Carmen's beautiful pussy lips, I didn't want to sample anything else. "I guess I want you. I want your attitude. Your spite. Your sass. I never thought I would want a woman like that. But then again, I've never met one—until now." My hand slid up her back until I found the clasp keeping her sexy bra in place. My fingers unfastened it, letting it come loose around her perfect nipples. I pulled the straps down, removing the material so I could see all the angles of her round, plump tits. Both of my hands palmed them, my fingers swiping over her nipples. "I've fucked virgin pussy, but nothing like yours."

Her hands rested against my chest, her fingers lightly touching my skin. She tilted her head at my statement. "I'm not a virgin, Bosco."

"You feel like one." She was so tight around my dick. She clamped down on me every time I was inside her, squeezing me tightly before she finally relaxed and allowed me deeper inside. Even when her body stopped clenching me, she still had the tightest cunt I'd ever had been in. "And you've never been properly fucked anyway, so you pretty much are." My fingers moved to the lace at her hips, and I felt the material against my callused fingertips. Topless, she sat on my lap, her shoulders back and her tits pointed at me like they were on display.

She watched me for a long time, like she thinking about something else. "So, what's your plan?"

"My plan?" I asked, having no idea what she was referring to.

"With me. Am I here to entertain you for a while before you lose interest?"

I found it hard to believe I would ever lose interest in her. "My intentions with you are none of your business."

"Oh, really?" she asked, challenging me with her clipped tone. "Because I'm looking for a husband and four kids. I'm getting that—regardless of your intentions."

I wasn't sure what she meant by that. "You want me to give you four kids?"

Her hands dragged down to my stomach, her eyes never leaving mine. "No. But I'm telling you that's going to happen regardless of what happens here. So hopefully, your interest doesn't last too long. I know mine won't."

And just like that, she made me even more obsessed than I already was. Every time she put me in my place, I admired her. This woman had a good head on her shoulders, wasn't afraid to show her ambition. She wanted a happily ever after and wasn't afraid to ask for it. "You're fond of that young boy?"

Her eyes narrowed in confusion as she took a moment to understand what I was referring to. "Luca?"

I gave a slight nod.

"He's my nephew. I adore him."

"Your nephew?" I asked. "I thought he was Mia's son." From the information I'd gathered, he was the son of some deadbeat loser in America. Carter had nothing to do with that and hadn't come into the picture until recently.

"He's Carter's son too," she said, a fire burning in her eyes. "Therefore, he's my nephew." With a hint of rage in her eyes, she stood her ground and declared her love for a boy she wasn't actually related to. "He's a sweet boy with a heart of gold. Being around him only reminds me how much I want a son of my own. It reminds me how much I want to be a mom. I know I'm young and have time to settle down...but sometimes I want to skip to that final chapter in my dating life. I see what Griffin and Vanessa have, and I want that for myself." A hopeless romantic, she wore her heart on her sleeve.

I would never give that to her, simply because I didn't possess a romantic bone in my body. I wouldn't take a wife, and I certainly wouldn't love a woman. All I understood were power, sex, and money. Nothing else mattered. Having a family sounded like a joke. I had my brother, and that was all I needed.

She gave me a look of pity. "You don't want that too? Someday?"

I held her gaze and never gave my answer—because I didn't need to.

"That's a shame." She pushed off my chest and rose to her feet before she pulled her panties down her long legs. Her sexy slit was visible, her pussy lips hypnotizing. Naked from head to toe, she was stunning.

She moved back to my lap and pulled my boxers and sweatpants down, releasing my twitching cock from my clothes. He was thick and ready to go, knowing she was wet all the way through.

She straddled my hips and caught the head of my cock between her lips. Slowly, she sank her body on top of me, pushing my head past the notch in her entrance and all the way in. Deeper she sank, moving until she was sitting right on my balls.

I closed my eyes and moaned, still not used to how incredible this pussy was. So wet and tight, it was the best cunt on this earth. I couldn't picture myself sliding through another pair of lips, not when this was the best there was. I could feel her warm wetness, the way she tightened around me initially and then released.

She breathed into my mouth, digging her nails into my shoulders as she tried to keep her moans at bay. She sat idle on my lap, just enjoying the feeling of my thick cock inside her. Her breath was taken away, and like she'd never had me before, she was overcome with the stark goodness. "Bosco..." We hadn't even started to move together yet, and her body was already shivering as every nerve fired off under her skin.

I planted my feet against the rug, my knees far apart. My hands glided up her perky ass and across her smooth back, my eyes on her tits. I could feel her squeezing me harder than usual, could feel the tremors under my fingertips. "Beautiful, how do I feel?" I tilted her head and forced her to look at me, seeing the truth in her eyes so she couldn't hide it.

"Perfect." She ground against me slightly but didn't

start to move. Her arms hooked around my neck, and she rubbed her nose against mine. "You make me feel so...full."

I slowly rocked against her, my cock moving through her wetness.

"You're so big. So thick. So right. I've never..." She closed her eyes and started to move.

"Never what?" I pressed, my fingers digging into her ass.

She opened her eyes again, her lips parted with her deep breathing. "Never had such good sex."

This wasn't new information to me. I knew I was the best she'd ever had—because I was the best every woman had.

"Never had such a big man."

I wanted to start fucking her, but I also wanted to hear every word she had to say. This queen was submitting to me willingly, telling me all the things I wanted to hear without asking.

"Never had such a strong man." She fisted the back of my hair before she kissed me, her lips shaking with passion. She started to move up and down, pushing her slit over my dick to the base before she rose again.

I dragged her pussy up and down as I kissed her, burying myself deep inside her and making it my permanent residence. She came all the way over here because she wanted the action. She could have any man she wanted, but she kept screwing a man she hated. Her lips trembled for me, her pussy constricted. She reached the clouds and hit heaven when I was inside her, knowing no other man would make her feel this high.

A woman wouldn't make me feel this high either.

I guided her up and down and enjoyed her fucking me, her sexy tits grazing against my chest as she moved. My feet pushed against the ground slightly as I raised my hips into her. I didn't have to do anything at all if I didn't want to—since this woman was doing all the fucking. I had the most beautiful woman in the world screwing me right on the couch, a woman who could have any man she wanted. With supermodel looks and the attitude of a queen, she was a woman a cut above the rest—but she was there with me.

She talked about her future husband and kids, not realizing they would never exist.

Because I would never let her go. Not now—not ever.

———

SHE LAY ON MY CHEST, HER TITS PRESSED AGAINST ME AND her body weightless. Her long hair was everywhere, spread across my chest, my arm, and my neck. Her shampoo smelled like vanilla, and her perfume smelled like cherries. One leg was wrapped around mine, and she was completely at peace, her entire body relaxed as we lay in my bed together.

I stared out the window and to the city beyond, looking at the beautiful lights that shone in the darkness. Tuscany was just beyond, a backdrop of darkness because there were so few lights. I wasn't tired because I was usually awake at this time of night, working at the casino. But Carmen was on a regular schedule, waking up early and going to bed at a reasonable hour.

My phone started to vibrate on my nightstand. It was Ronan.

It was probably important, so I shifted her off me without waking her, then got out of bed. I grabbed the phone and walked into the living room before I took the call. "What's up, Ronan?"

"We've got a problem. Just found out one of the guys skimmed a chip."

A chip in the casino was worth ten thousand dollars —basically nothing.

"The cameras caught him sliding it into his pocket, taking it from the dealer when he looked away for a nanosecond. Since it's such a small offense, I'm not sure what to do. It's not like he tried to clean out an entire drawer."

I walked to the floor-to-ceiling window, standing in my boxers and looking down at the city I owned. It didn't matter if it was one chip or a million—he broke the law. "He goes in the ring."

Ronan was quiet for a moment. "He's got two kids."

"Don't give a shit. Everyone knows the rules. He was aware of the ramifications when he paid his membership."

"Maybe we can just give him a warning—"

"No." I clenched my jaw, furious that my brother was

too soft for his own good. "Every crime is punished to the same degree. It keeps everyone in line. It's the only thing stopping pandemonium from breaking out. If you want these men to respect us, they need to fear us. No crime is excusable. I don't give a shit if he stole a penny or a million dollars. I don't care that his kids will be orphans. If he gave a damn about his family, he wouldn't have risked everything for a goddamn chip."

Ronan didn't have a rebuttal.

"I'll take care of this if you can't." It was vital that this casino ran under my authority. I was known as a blood-thirsty psychopath—and that was how I liked it.

"I can—"

"I'll be down there in ten minutes. He's going in the ring. We've got another man waiting for his chance."

"Bosco, the guy is in his fifties."

"Again, does it sound like I care?" If men wanted to fuck with me, I would fuck with them back. He would die for his stupidity, and I wouldn't lose any sleep over it. "No one gets a slap on the wrist. No one gets a warning. Stealing is punishable by death." I hung up and ground my teeth together, annoyed Ronan didn't have the balls of steel that I possessed. He was far more empathetic, especially when a guy had kids. Since we'd lost our mother, he'd been particularly sensitive to the matter.

But I didn't give a shit.

Her beautiful voice broke the silence. "Everything alright?"

I turned to look at her, to see her standing in a t-shirt

I'd left on the floor. Though the material was shapeless, it didn't stop her from looking far sexier than she did in the lingerie she wore earlier. For a brief moment, I forgot how angry I was. "I have to go to the casino. I'll be back in a few hours." I tossed the phone on the table as I headed back toward the hallway.

"Is everything okay?" With sleepy eyes and a relaxed posture, she looked like she was ready to go right back to bed.

"No." I picked her up on my way, wrapping her legs around my waist as I carried her back to the bedroom. I laid her on the sheets before I grabbed my jeans and long-sleeved shirt. "Go back to sleep. I'll be back before you wake up."

"You want me to stay here?" she asked with surprise.

"Yes." I pulled the shirt over my head and then got my jeans on.

"What happened?" she asked, sitting up.

"An asshole crossed me. Ronan is too much of a pussy to do anything about it, so I have to take care of it."

"What did he do?" she asked.

"He stole a chip from one of the tables. Now I have to put him in the ring."

Her eyes widened with horror. "You're going to make him fight to the death for stealing one chip?"

I wasn't in the mood for her opinions. I stared her down with a formidable look, warning her now wasn't the time for her attitude. "It doesn't matter if it's one chip or a thousand. He knows the law—and he broke it."

"Are you sure it wasn't an accident?"

"Yes."

"So if I piss you off, are you going to throw me in the ring too?" she asked hesitantly.

"No, Beautiful. Women aren't members of the casino."

"That's sexist."

I gave her a dark look, giving her another warning.

This time, she went quiet.

"Go back to bed." I turned away and headed down the hallway.

Her footsteps sounded behind me as she followed me.

I grabbed my jacket from the coatrack, along with my phone and wallet. I hit the button for the elevator and typed in the code so the gated doors would open.

"Bosco."

I turned around, still wearing a scowl.

She moved into me and wrapped her arms around my neck. She rose on her tiptoes and kissed me goodbye, giving me the softest embrace with those full lips. It wasn't a kiss intended to drag me back to bed, but it was a kiss that told me she was worried about me. "Be careful."

All the rage I felt for the situation disappeared when I looked at her. A soft grin spread over my lips, seeing the way she was slowly becoming attached me, the way she wanted me to come back in the same condition I left. "Beautiful, are you worried about me?" My hand slid into her hair as I cradled her face, seeing a new side to her that she'd tried to keep hidden from me for so long.

She didn't make a smartass comment to bury the truth. She finally dropped her bullshit attitude and gave it to me straight. "Don't let it go to your head, alright?"

I grinned wider. "It already has."

11

CARMEN

I DIDN'T SLEEP WELL while he was gone. Normally, I was out like a light, the night passing within a heartbeat. But now, I tossed and turned, slightly conscious as I felt his cool sheets freezing my skin. The heater was on and it was at least twenty degrees warmer inside than it was outside, but I was still frozen to the bone.

I was starting to become dependent on his heat.

When his heavy footsteps pounded against the hard-wood floor again, I finally felt comfortable for the first time since he'd left. I heard his clothes drop to the floor, and then his heavy weight hit the bed.

Already knowing exactly what he wanted, I lay on my back and opened my legs, giving him ample room to move over my body and position himself on top of me.

Without uttering a single word, he folded my knees toward my chest and thrust himself hard inside me with one movement.

"Oh..." My hand dug into his hair, and my arm hooked around his back.

He buried his face in my neck as he started to fuck me, giving me a quick but lazy screw. He breathed hard against my skin as he pounded into me hard, driving me into a climax as quickly as he could so he could finish.

It was a great way for him to announce his presence.

After he shoved every drop of his come inside me, he turned over and lay on his back, his eyes immediately closed like he was ready to go to sleep immediately. His muscular frame heated the sheets instantly, making me feel warm now that he'd chased away the cold.

It hit me then that I was sleeping beside the dictator of the city, a man who possessed more wealth than anyone else I'd ever heard of. He went down to his casino in the middle of the night to sentence a man to death.

That was an immense kind of power.

And I was sleeping with him.

I moved into his side and wrapped my arm around his muscular waist. My head rested on his shoulder, and I hooked my leg between his.

He wrapped his thick arm around me, his lips resting against my hairline.

"So...someone died tonight?"

"Yes." He said it without remorse, the calmest he'd ever been.

"And you watched it?"

"I always watch. You can't sentence a man to death

without watching the execution. It's a requirement of any leader."

I had a cast-iron stomach, but I wouldn't be able to swallow that. "So they just...beat each other with their fists?"

"If they're smart, they'll break an arm or a leg first so they can crush their skull." Bosco said it simply, like we were discussing what to make for dinner.

The heat provided suddenly wasn't enough, and I felt ice-cold. Bosco wasn't the man making the killing blow, but he ordered death just like he ordered a drink—as if it was of no consequence. His lust for violence and lack of empathy terrified me because they were traits of a psychopath. My body automatically moved away from him, my instinct for survival kicking in. I pulled the sheets back then sat up, the adrenaline heavy in my veins. "I want to go home."

He sighed quietly from his place on the bed, absolutely still like he had no intention of moving.

I grabbed my clothes off the floor and hurriedly pulled them on, eager to get out of there as quickly as possible. I hated waiting for him to give me permission, but since I didn't have the code to the elevator, I was at his mercy.

I was powerless.

He finally sat up in bed and looked at me. "I would never hurt you."

Those words meant nothing to me. "I want to leave."

I stayed at the foot of the bed so I wasn't within arm's reach.

"Beautiful—"

"Why won't you let me leave?" I demanded. "I'm not a dog that you own. I'm a fucking human being, and you have no right to keep me locked in here. When a lady says she wants to go home, you do what she says. Now let me out, or I'll break through the window." My courage stemmed from my fear, along with a rush of the adrenaline. I feared I would never get out of there, that I'd lost my rights a long time ago.

He continued to sit there, watching me with disappointment.

I lost my patience and stormed into his living room and picked up the chair from the dining table. I prepared to throw it through the window and watch it shatter into a million pieces. We were at least a dozen stories high, but there had to be a fire escape somewhere.

"Beautiful." He snatched the chair out of my hands and put it back on the floor. "Knock it off."

"You knock it off."

"You want to leave? Fine." He grabbed me by the wrist and pulled me to the elevator. "Here's the code. Five. Seven. Four. Three. Eight. Five. That's the master code. You can come and go whenever you want." He hit the numbers on the pad, and the doors opened to the elevator.

I finally stopped panicking.

He stared at me with a clenched jaw, clearly furious

at my explosion. "You can take the elevator to the lobby and tell one of my men to take you home. Or you can calm down and come back to bed with me. I would never hurt you, Carmen. Ever."

I looked away, unable to meet his fiery gaze anymore.

His chest continued to rise and fall rapidly, barely able to hold on to his rage. He was livid, judging by the way his closed fists caused the thick cords to strain. "I've never raised a hand to a woman my entire life."

"But you have no problem killing someone because they took a single chip."

"It doesn't matter how much they stole. They took something that belonged to me—and they face the consequences. If they cared that much about their mortality, they would keep their hands in their pockets. It's pretty simple. I don't comb the streets looking for victims to slaughter. I lay out my rules perfectly clearly to every member of my casino. The consequences are the same for everyone—regardless of the extent of the crime. It's earned me great respect, which keeps everyone in line. You can criticize my decisions all you want, but only a truly powerful man can sit in my seat and rule a kingdom smoothly."

I still wouldn't look at him.

He sighed again. "I won't apologize for being the man that I am. You come around my dick because you can feel the power in my veins. You get wet knowing you're fucking the most powerful man in this city. Don't pretend otherwise. But with great power comes great responsibility. If you aren't woman enough to handle that, then maybe you aren't woman enough to handle me." He slammed his hand onto the button, making the doors open again because they'd closed at some point during our conversation.

He turned away and marched back to his bedroom, the sound of his footsteps growing fainter as he disappeared down the hallway and back to bed.

Now I had the security code so I could leave whenever I wanted. He gave me a form of freedom, proving to me that I had some kind of power over him. But then his power dominated mine because I was still standing there.

All I had to do was walk inside the elevator and go home.

But I stood there, watching the doors shut for a second time. I could be on my way home right now, but I lingered, thinking about that warm bed with that hot man between the sheets. One moment, I hated him, and then the next, I wanted him even more than I did before. I was repulsed by his power but also drawn to it at the same time. I told myself I didn't need a man for anything, but now I was getting comfortable with his strength. I liked knowing I was invincible because he had control of everyone in this city. It gave me a sense of safety I hadn't even felt at my childhood home. I was raised by a strong man, and I was used to that luxury. Maybe deep down inside, I wanted that in a man...someone with unquestionable strength.

I turned around and did my greatest walk of shame, heading back to the bedroom where he was waiting for me. I was a slave without a chain. I was obedient without punishment. My brain told me to run for the hills, but the rest of my body knew this was the safest place I would ever be.

In his arms.

He was sitting up in bed waiting for me, the sheets pulled to his waist. He wore a dark expression, like my return wasn't enough to please him. His broad shoulders were tense with his anger, his biceps chiseled and defined. His arms rested by his sides, and despite his calm posture, he seemed inherently dangerous.

I slowly crept toward the bed, moving slowly like he was a wild dog that might bite me.

His eyes followed me the entire time.

I stopped by the bedside and undressed, dropping my sweater, jeans, and then my undergarments.

He watched every single move.

Despite all the shame inside my chest, I pulled back the sheets and got back into bed beside him. He was the most dangerous person in this city, but I somehow felt safer once his body was beside mine. My head hit the pillow and I looked at the ceiling, feeling his rough gaze on my cheek.

He suddenly moved, like he'd been waiting for the perfect moment to trap me. He maneuvered his heavy body on top of mine, and even though we'd just screwed twenty minutes ago, his cock was hard and inside me instantly.

I clawed at him, instantly feeling safe once we were combined together.

He held his face above mine, possession in his eyes. "I knew you wouldn't leave."

I WAS WORKING AT THE SHOP WHEN GRIFFIN AND VANESSA walked inside. I was grateful that Bosco didn't make his surprise visits anymore, because if these two men were in the same room together, no one would survive.

I knew Vanessa hadn't told Griffin anything because he didn't look remotely angry.

I knew I could trust her.

"Hey, what are you guys doing here?" I smiled from behind the counter, seeing Vanessa show off her small baby bump in her long-sleeved shirt. She wore a jacket on top, but it was open, revealing the slight extension. She was almost early in her second trimester, but she was showing so well because she had such a petite frame.

Griffin stayed behind her, always having her in front of him so he could keep an eye on her.

"We had a doctor's appointment," Vanessa said. "Griffin took the day off so he could take me."

"Hope everything went well," I said.

"Yeah, everything is great," Vanessa said. "The baby is

doing well. Just had a routine checkup. Nothing to worry about. So we wanted to see if you had time to get lunch." Vanessa pretended our last conversation never happened, like I didn't tell her I was sleeping with the most notorious criminal in southern Italy.

"I'm always free for lunch." I grabbed my jacket and purse, and we left the shop to head to a bistro just a few blocks away. Vanessa was craving pasta, and since she got to choose whatever she wanted, that's where we stopped.

The three of us sat together at a table and ordered.

Griffin wasn't talkative, but then again, he never was. He wasn't indifferent toward me or cold. He just didn't have a lot to say.

"I can't believe Carter and Mia are finally getting married," Vanessa said. "She told me she picked up her dress."

"Yeah, I picked up Luca while they were in Milan. It's weird seeing my brother so grown up. He was such a selfish jerk before, and now he's a whole new man. It took some time getting used to, but now I've finally come to accept it. He's matured a lot."

"Mia definitely made him into a better man," Vanessa said. "A good woman will do that." She glanced at Griffin.

He held her gaze with such intensity that he could burn the whole place down.

I looked away, feeling like I was intruding on something intimate.

"Anyway," Vanessa said. "I'm excited for them. Seems like your parents really like Mia."

"They do. She's very sweet. I also think my parents are just relieved Carter found someone."

Vanessa chuckled. "Come on, he's not that bad."

"We both know he can be a pain sometimes."

"Sometimes," she said. "But not often."

The food arrived, and we ate quietly. Griffin still hadn't said anything, but that wasn't unusual for him.

I knew Vanessa was eager to talk about Bosco, but she wouldn't mention it in front of her husband. I wasn't stupid enough to admit it either.

After we finished eating, Griffin excused himself from the table. "I'll be waiting outside. I know when I'm not wanted." He leaned down and kissed her on the forehead before he stepped outside and stood near the window, wearing nothing but a t-shirt and jeans. The cold had no effect on him at all—a lot like Bosco.

Vanessa glanced at him through the window then turned back to me. "For a man, he's highly intuitive."

"Thanks for not telling him."

"You know me. I can keep a secret. So…what's going on with him? Did you end things?"

I was stuck even deeper than I was before. "No…"

"Oh no. What happened?"

"I don't know… Every time I pull away, I get sucked back in. Just last night, I stormed out of his bedroom and demanded to leave. He typed in the security code so I could take the elevator…but then I went back to bed."

She shook her head slightly. "Girl, you have it bad."

"I don't understand it. I know he's not the right man for me...but I can't leave."

"The sex must be unbelievable."

"It's so good that I don't think I could have sex with anyone else anyway." The idea of meeting a new man and taking him back to my place sounded pointless. He would get off, and then I would touch myself after he left because he couldn't get the job done. Then I would think about Bosco, missing him while my fingers worked my clit. "He told me one of the men at his casino stole a single chip, so he put him in the ring and made him fight some other guy to the death. He lost...and Bosco acts like this is perfectly normal."

"It's crazy."

"It just terrifies me. He told me he would never hurt me...and I feel stupid for believing him."

"He never has, right?" she asked.

"Never." I never even suspected he might. Sometimes, he became angry, but the most he ever did was press me into a wall and kiss me so hard that I forgot why I was pissed in the first place. "We have this chemistry... I can't explain it."

"You don't need to explain it." She glanced at Griffin out the window, where he continued to stand there and survey the street as people came and went. "Trust me, I get it. But if you really don't see a future with this guy, you have to get out now. It's only going to get worse."

I agreed with everything she said. The longer I

waited, the more difficult it would be. It'd only been a few weeks, and I was in so deep already. I was calling him and asking to see him. I was coming by his apartment and riding him on the couch. I was telling him I missed him...and meant it. I was sleeping with him every night and actually enjoying it. "I know..."

"I'm sorry, girl."

"I know you are. Being around Luca just reminds me how much I want a family. It doesn't need to happen tomorrow or next year. But it'll never happen with Bosco, and I never want it to. I'm stuck sleeping with a man when I should be looking for my husband."

"I agree. But I think finding Mr. Right is the least of your problems right now. Right now, you're dating the scariest man in this city. This guy is so strong that our family is powerless to stand up to him. If he wanted to take you and never give you back, we wouldn't be able to do anything about it. Even Griffin can't do anything. No matter if Griffin rounded up all his contacts, Bosco still has this entire city under his thumb."

"I know..."

"So, end it. Do it quickly, and don't look back."

Easier said than done.

"Do you think he'll let you go?" she asked, a hint of fear in her voice.

I really had no idea. "He said he would never hurt me."

"He may not think keeping you against your will falls into that category."

She was right. "When I asked to leave the other night, he gave me the security code and walked away. I could take the elevator to the lobby and have one of his men drive me home."

"That's not the same thing, Carmen."

I knew it wasn't, but I hoped that momentary taste of freedom was an indicator.

"What are you going to do if he doesn't cooperate?"

I'd turned him down a few times in the beginning, but that only seemed to make him want me more. If I walked away altogether, that might ignite his lust in a dangerous way. It might make him possess me harder, make his grip so tight that I would never know freedom ever again. "I don't think there's anything I can do."

12

BOSCO

I was in my office when Ronan stepped inside.

"What is it?" I asked, hardly looking up at him.

"The family is here to claim the body." His throat shifted when he finished talking, and there was a slight look of resentment in his eyes. He still didn't agree with my decision, and he didn't hesitate to show his disapproval.

Like I gave a damn. "Hand it over."

He sat in the leather chair facing my desk, like this conversation wasn't over.

"Yes?" I looked up again, this time giving him my complete attention.

"I heard the men talking. You're seeing someone." He gave me a look of accusation, as if he was offended I hadn't confided in him with this information.

"Correction. I'm fucking someone."

"You never fuck the same woman twice. So what's this about?"

I wouldn't be annoyed with his question if he didn't question my decisions so often. "I'm not sure. I met her a few weeks ago. She was about to get raped in an alleyway, and I intervened. She's been showing her gratitude ever since."

"Is it getting serious?"

I didn't do relationships and I didn't consider Carmen to be my girlfriend, but she had my fidelity as well as my complete obsession. "I'm not gonna marry the woman. But we're monogamous. Hope that answers your question."

Both of his eyebrows rose almost off his face. "You're exclusive? Then it's damn serious."

"If that's how you want to describe it..."

"Maybe I should meet her."

"Maybe not," I said coldly. "Give it a few more weeks. We're working out a few bugs right now."

"What?" he teased. "She hates you?"

"Actually, yes." I didn't hide my grin. "She despises me. But she wants me anyway."

"This sounds like an interesting relationship."

"Quite."

"Could this be love?" he asked, teasing me again.

"Not even close. It's lust—which is far stronger. Now, if we're finished with the gossip, you should get back to work."

His mood immediately soured. "I get that you're an

asshole to most people because you have to be. But when it's just the two of us in your office, it's overdone."

I had no idea where this was coming from. Our relationship was the same as it always had been There was nothing special about my words that could have possibly provoked him. I was so caught off guard by what he said, I didn't have a comeback.

"You haven't been the same since Mom died. It's like you died too. And I'm fucking sick of it." His voice rose louder as he kept talking. "I get that the two of you were a little closer than she and I were, but it's been five years. You need to let it go and move on." He marched out of my office and slammed the door behind him.

I barely had a moment to reflect on what he'd said before Drake stepped inside. "What?" I asked, in a darker mood than I had been before.

"It's about Carmen. Or should I come back later...?" My one-word answer was enough to put him on edge. Now was definitely not a good time.

But since it was about Carmen, I wanted to know every detail. "What about her?"

"She had lunch with Vanessa again."

This oughta be good. "Yes?"

"Vanessa told her to end things with you...and Carmen agreed."

After the way she'd crawled back into my bed, she actually thought she would have the strength to walk away from me? I found that very unlikely, but it pissed me off that she was even considering the idea. "Did she say when?"

"No. But she thinks she should stay away from you."

Yes. She should have stayed away from me. She never should have ended up in that alleyway. She wouldn't have met me at all, and she would be living a normal life right now. Maybe she would have met a nice man to become her husband. But that would never happen now.

Because she was mine. "That'll be all, Drake."

"Sir." He nodded before he walked out.

13

CARMEN

I'D NEVER BEEN SO nervous in my life.

But I was utterly terrified.

Bosco was an unpredictable man. I had no idea what his reaction might be, but judging by the fact that he'd let a man die in the most brutal way possible, it wouldn't be good. He had a frozen heart in his hollow chest. He didn't see me as a person, but a piece of property, no different from the watch that sat on his wrist.

Regardless of what his reaction was, this wouldn't be a clean break.

He wouldn't let me go easily.

I never realized how much I needed my family until that moment. A part of me wanted to run to my father and ask for his help. In any other situation, he would be able to fix it for me. He would be able to protect me.

But both he and my uncle couldn't do a damn thing.

Even Griffin, the strongest man I'd ever known, was useless.

The most powerful man in the world was my opponent. And I would never win this war.

We didn't talk for a few days after I left. I thought I could use the space and time to collect my thoughts, to consider how I was going to accomplish this. The distance would allow me to think clearly, to stop thinking with the nerve center between my legs and starting thinking with that big brain of mine.

But waiting only made it worse.

Only made me more afraid.

I was sitting at the dining table drinking an entire bottle of wine by myself while staring at my phone. I kept going over the words in my head, trying to think of the right way to phrase it. If I acted timid or scared, he would run me into the ground. I had to be confident and strong. The smartest thing to do was to do it over the phone, not because I was a coward, but because he couldn't touch me that way. He couldn't push me up against a wall and shut me up with a fat kiss.

I took another long drink and finally made the call.

He picked up right after the first ring. "Beautiful." His deep, masculine voice was like perfectly aged wine. It was so smooth, full of texture, and it was bold. Just his voice was sexy, as sexy as his hands felt against my tits. He had the kind of voice made to speak to a woman, to make her wet without being in the same room with her.

Listening to him destroyed all of my resolve. Like the

weak person I was, I instantly succumbed to desire, my thighs pressing together under the table. My heart rate spiked, and I couldn't drink any more wine because my stomach started to tighten.

He didn't say anything else, perfectly comfortable with the silence.

I wished I were just as unaffected by tension as he was. "I want to talk to you about something…"

"You do?" he asked, slightly amused. "What would that be?" There was a playful hint to his tone, but there was also an underlying vibration of hostility. Without even stating it, it seemed like he was threatening me. He was volatile, dancing between rage and amusement. He could project so much with so little.

As if he were standing right in front of me, he knocked me off-balance again. I had to recover by taking a long pause, using the silence as a crutch. I reminded myself that I had to be stern. I had to match his hostility with mine, make him listen to me because he respected me. "This is over, Bosco." I kept my tone surprisingly strong, like it wasn't even my voice that was speaking. "I'm done with you."

His reaction was instant because he didn't need a moment to pause. "Beautiful…" He chuckled over the line as he said my nickname, like my words were nothing but comical to him. "Be careful what you say next."

I was afraid that he didn't take me seriously at all, that I was the one dumping him, and he was the one making the threats. "You asked me to give you a chance, and I did. You aren't right for me. I know what I'm looking for...and you aren't it."

"That's ironic. Considering you're exactly what I'm looking for..."

My heart started to race quicker, started to beat like a heavy drum. "I'm being serious, Bosco. I don't want to see you anymore."

"I know you're being serious." His tone began to deepen, began to turn darker and more sinister. "But I don't care." Without another word, he hung up and the line went dead.

I dropped my phone on the table and watched his name disappear from the screen. As if I could hear his footsteps from down the hall, I knew he was approaching. It was only a matter of minutes before he arrived. What would happen when he got there, I had no idea.

But it wouldn't be good.

HE GOT PAST MY LOCKS WITHOUT EFFORT THEN STEPPED into my apartment, wearing a long-sleeved fitted shirt and black jeans. His shiny watch was on his wrist, his hair was neatly combed, and he looked like the most terrifying and beautiful man I'd ever seen.

The whole bottle of wine wasn't enough to chase away the fear.

I was terrified.

I'd never been more afraid of anyone in my life.

He moved across the dining room until he pulled out the chair across from me. He sat down and faced me, his eyes hinting at the rage circulating in his veins that very moment. He was pissed but doing his best to keep it bottled deep inside.

I had to stick to my guns. I couldn't give up. So I looked him in the eye and crossed my arms over my chest. "I meant what I said, and I won't change my mind."

"I'm not here to change your mind." The cryptic message was impossible to decipher, but it was filled with such a heavy level of threat that it stopped my heart from beating. We'd just crossed into new territory, a place I'd never wanted to visit. "I'm here to tell you how this is going to be from now on."

"How what's gonna be?" My voice started to shake even though I did my best to control it.

"I was hoping it wouldn't come to this." A slight smile was on his lips. "After you talked to Vanessa the first time, I thought I'd straightened you out. I proved how much you needed me...how much you wanted me. Then you spoke to her a second time..."

My heart convulsed in terror when I realized he knew everything, spied on every conversation I had with anyone. I didn't even realize one of his men tailed me everywhere I went because they were disguised so well. They even eavesdropped on my conversations, which meant they were within ten feet of me at all times. The idea made my body shiver, but not in a good way.

"I thought you would come to your senses again... and realize it would be the biggest mistake of your life." He shook his head slightly, his look full of disappointment. "But you chose wrong."

My arms tightened around my chest, and I swallowed the lump in my throat. I'd been backed into a corner by this man, and there was nowhere for me to run. The police would ignore my calls, and if I called my family, they would all die.

Bosco kept his ice-cold stare on me. "You never gave me a real chance."

Now my voice was hardly audible. "Yes, I did..."

"If that were the case, we wouldn't be having this conversation. I'm everything you want in a man—powerful, rich, and good in bed. You won't find a better man out there, and we both know it."

"There are lots of better men out there..."

"If that were the case, you would be able to fight me. But you can't. Let's not pretend that you aren't utterly terrified of me, that I could wipe out your entire family with a slight nod to my men."

My hands were shaking because I was so scared.

"You want me in your bed every night. You want me to sleep on my chest because it's your favorite place. You want to keep walking the streets with your invincibility. The only reason you're doing this is because you're afraid of me...even though I told you I would never hurt you."

"You just threatened to kill my family," I whispered.

"And that would hurt me more than anything else in the world."

He stared at me with those intense eyes, eyes so cold they reminded me of the Arctic. He sat perfectly upright, his shirt fitting his body like a glove. He was a man of muscle, built like a racehorse. "But I would never lay a hand on you. And I would have no motivation to hurt your family if you give me what I want."

"What about what I want?" I demanded.

He cocked his head slightly. "I am what you want."

"I don't want a murderer."

"And I don't murder people."

"But you cast the death sentence, which makes you just as bad."

"Really?" he asked. "So the judges in America who put criminals on death row...are they murderers?"

"Not the same thing."

"It's exactly the same thing, Beautiful. I own this city, so I'm the judge, the jury, and the people. I control all things because I'm the only one who can. Some people die. Some people live. It's just how it goes. If people followed the rules, there would be no need for punishment. Unfortunately, people are just too stupid for that."

I had no idea what to say. No idea what to do.

"If you were some other woman, I would let you go without a fight. But you're very special to me. And I know I'm special to you. You want to run from me, but by my side is the safest place you'll ever be."

"Then why do I feel so scared?" I whispered.

"You aren't scared of me," he said confidently. "You're scared of the way you feel about me."

Maybe that was partially true, but I would never admit it.

"So this is how it's going to be." He rested his hands on the table and leaned toward me, his hard jaw clenched because he was still annoyed. "You're going to tell Vanessa that you broke it off with me. I let you go. In reality, you'll be packing your things and coming to live with me. And instead of being a woman I'm casually seeing, you'll be mine exclusively. You'll share my bed every night. You'll be the woman on my arm. In exchange, I'll offer you anything you could possibly want. Any car you want, any set of diamonds, any—"

"I don't want your money. I told you it doesn't impress me."

"Then what do you want, Beautiful?" he whispered.

"My freedom."

"You can't have that—"

"Fuck. You." I rose to my feet and snatched the empty bottle, prepared to slam it over his head.

His eyes narrowed at my outburst, but he still seemed slightly amused by my words.

"Who the fuck do you think you are?" I demanded. "You think you can just do whatever—"

"Yes."

"Well, you can't do that with me. I don't care about the men outside this apartment or how much money you have. I'm not a slave, and I refused to be a slave. I will not come quietly. I will not submit willingly. I will not give up on the life that I deserve—"

"Then let me give you the life you deserve." He slowly rose to his feet and came close to me, his eyes shifting back and forth between mine. "I told you I would give you anything. You want a husband and four kids? Fine, I'll give that to you."

"You'll let me marry another man?" I asked incredulously.

"No." He took hold of the back my neck, touching me gently. "I'll be your husband. I'll give you four kids. Problem solved."

My eyes flashed in shock. "You're crazy."

"I'm compromising with you. That's the one thing you want, and I'm giving it to you."

I pushed his arm away. "No."

He lowered his hand and didn't try to grab me again. "We can do this the easy way or the hard way. Trust me, you don't want to do it the hard way."

"You know me, Bosco," I said coldly. "I'll always take the high road. I don't accept this, and I never will. I don't want to be involved with a man like you. You kill people—"

"And you think Bones is any better? He killed people for a living, and now he's your family. What about Conway and Carter? Buying women from the Underground? What about your father and uncle? Running one of the biggest weapons companies in Europe. And you're gonna sit there and say what I do is wrong? Fucking hypocrite."

I was speechless because there was no argument against that. He had me cornered.

"You want me, Carmen. I see it in your eyes every time your legs are spread and you're underneath me. I feel it in the way you kiss me. I feel it in the way you come around my dick. Stop pretending otherwise."

"Yes, I like sleeping with you. But that doesn't mean I want more from you."

"That's too bad," he said coldly. "Because you're getting more from me."

"I refuse," I said quietly. "I refuse."

"You don't get to refuse. If you do, I don't need to tell you everything I'll do to your family. I'll wipe them all out at the same time, send a hundred men to each place and destroy your family legacy like that." He snapped his fingers.

Just the thought made me want to burst into tears.

"Don't call my bluff, Carmen. It's not a gamble you'll win."

I had no choice. I would rather die than let anything happen to the people I loved, so I would submit. They would do the same for me in a heartbeat. "I have a compromise..."

He chuckled, like the suggestion was ridiculous. "You don't get to make compromises."

"Look, I'll give you what you want. I'll cooperate fully. But there has to be a timetable on this."

He narrowed his eyes at my suggestion.

"You get what you want, and I get what I want."

It was the first time he didn't have anything to say.

"I'll be yours for...a month. But when that time is up, I get to walk away. I'm a good person who deserves to find happiness. My husband is out there somewhere, and we're supposed to have a family together. I'm not giving up on that. Not ever. But I won't risk my family either. You're going to give that to me."

"Why would I agree to that when I could have you forever?"

It was a long shot and a low blow, but I was out of ideas. I had to find a way out of this. Otherwise, I was dooming myself forever. "Because your mother would be ashamed of you."

My words hit the mark, and his eyes narrowed, but not in anger. Like my shot struck the center of his heart, he staggered back slightly, wounded by the bullet that pierced his flesh. There were very few moments that made him seem human, and those moments usually happened when he spoke of his mother.

"One month."

He slowly recovered from the blow. "Six."

"Three."

His eyes narrowed on my face, considering the offer I had put on the table. He was quiet for so long it seemed like he was going to reject it. But finally, he gave the answer I wanted to hear. "Three."

Printed in Great Britain
by Amazon